CARRIE AND HOPE

By the Author

Emily's Art and Soul

Before Now

No Regrets

Carrie and Hope

CARRIE AND HOPE

by

Joy Argento

2021

CARRIE AND HOPE
© 2021 By Joy Argento. All Rights Reserved.

ISBN 13: 978-1-63555-827-2

This Trade Paperback Original Is Published By
Bold Strokes Books, Inc.
P.O. Box 249
Valley Falls, NY 12185

First Edition: February 2021

Credits
Editor: Cindy Cresap
Production Design: Susan Ramundo
Cover Design By Tammy Seidick
Cover Art By Joy Argento

Lyrics from Safe Hands (©2004), Run (©2003) and Saint Jude (©2006) composed by Leah Zicari and published by Guitarlily Music. Used by permission. All rights reserved. Available at iTunes and YouTube.

Dedication

This book is dedicated to
my newest grandson, Grayson.
He has been the light that has gotten me
through the darkness of 2020.

Acknowledgments

I can't dedicate this book to one grandson without mentioning my other three loves, Hayden, Matthew, and Ban. I love you all. If I had known how wonderful it is to have grandchildren I would have skipped over parenthood and jumped right to being a grandparent. I'm just kidding. My three kids, Jamie, Jess and Tony, mean the world to me.

Thanks to my wonderful editor, Cindy Cresap. I learn more and more from you with each book. I appreciate you.

Extra special thanks to Leah Zicari for letting me use her song lyrics as the poems in this book. Check her music out at iTunes, cdbaby.com, YouTube, and her Facebook page, Leah Zicari Music and Theater.

"Safe Hands" Copyright ©2004 Leah Zicari, used by permission.

"Run" Copyright ©2003 Leah Zicari, used by permission.

"Saint Jude" Copyright ©2006 Leah Zicari, used by permission.

Tobie Hewitt and Susan Carmen-Duffy…I know your names. Thank you for all your support.

Thank you to anyone that has taken the time to read my books, emailed me, or put up a review. I appreciate each and every one of you.

CHAPTER ONE

"So, what do you think, Gram?" Carrie squeezed a little more moisturizing lotion out of the small tube and rubbed her hands together to warm it. The rich smell of spicy vanilla filled the room, displacing the smell of disinfectant in the air.

She picked up her grandmother's hand and gently worked the lotion into her skin. Eleanor Brice's hand looked all of its seventy-four years. Blue veins were visible through the thin skin, that was speckled with brown age spots. Her face, however, belied her age. She could have easily passed for a woman ten or fifteen years younger.

Sunlight poured in through two large windows and fell gracefully onto pastel green walls. Carrie, still dressed in her Dockers and button-down shirt from work, sat in the only chair in the room, pulled up next to the hospital bed. A tall dresser and two small tables, one on each side of the headboard, littered the sparsely furnished room.

"I am only telling this to you, Gram." Carrie leaned forward a little in her chair and lowered her voice, even though no one else was in the room. "I'm sure everyone else would think it's premature, but I think it might help." *At least I hope it helps.* "I don't know what else to do or where else to go to help me figure this out." Carrie began working on her grandmother's other hand with a fresh dab of lotion.

"I know what you are thinking. You think I can just talk to Mom about this. Right? Well, just between you and me," Carrie said, "I think Mom is in major denial." She placed her grandmother's hand gently on the bed and placed her hand over it. "Talking to her doesn't work. I think she is feeling just as lost about this as I am, but she won't admit it."

"How is our favorite resident?" Marge, one of the aides, asked Carrie as she entered the room. She was much older than most of the aides at the nursing home. Carrie guessed her to be in her mid-forties. Most of the aides looked to be barely out of high school.

"How are you doing today, Mrs. Brice?" Marge addressed Carrie's grandmother directly as she pulled her blanket down on the bed a little and folded it over.

"The same," Carrie answered. "We were having a nice little chat."

"You are such a good granddaughter. Visiting so often. I'm sure she appreciates it."

Marge always seemed somehow kinder and gentler than the younger aides. Carrie was always grateful when she was on duty.

"How are you today, Marge?" Carrie asked. They had chatted on other occasions when Carrie had visited Sunnyside Nursing Home.

"Can't complain. No one wants to hear it anyway," she said with a laugh. She pushed a chunk of her short red hair away from her eyes and adjusted the black-rimmed glasses farther up on her nose.

Carrie brought her attention back to her grandmother. "Do you think she hears anything I'm saying to her?" Carrie had asked the doctors at the hospital as well as several of the staff members at the nursing home this same question.

Her grandmother had been a healthy, active senior citizen just three months ago, living in her own apartment in Hill Manor Senior Apartments. She still did her own cooking and cleaning, rarely needing help with anything. A slip and fall in her bathroom caused the coma that stilled her vivacity, a feeding tube, the only thing standing between life and death.

Carrie had been at her grandmother's bedside every day after work, and every weekend, in the first few weeks after the accident. Now, she tried to come at least every other day. It was starting to wear on her and make her feel much older than her thirty-four years.

"I would like to think she hears and understands every word you say. But I really don't know, Miss Martin."

"Please call me Carrie." They'd been through this before. Carrie suspected by Marge's southern accent that calling her *Miss* was a habit that was hard for her to break.

"Anything I can get for you, *Carrie*? A cup of coffee? We have a fresh pot at the nurses' station." She fussed a little more with the blankets.

Carrie shook her head. Her hair swept across her shoulders as she did, making her keenly aware that it hung down longer than she normally wore it. She just hadn't bothered to take the time to get it cut since her grandmother's accident. "No, thank you. I'm all set."

Marge nodded and quietly slipped out of the room, softly closing the door behind her. Carrie was once again alone with her grandmother. And her thoughts.

She brushed a stray piece of gray hair from her grandmother's forehead. "So, where was I? Oh yeah, I found a group that meets tomorrow night. It's close by here in fact. I know most people would think joining a grief support group would be a stupid idea, but, Gram, I miss you and I feel like even though you're here and still breathing," Carrie brushed a tear as it escaped and rolled down her cheek, "well, I just feel like I've lost you and I miss you. I don't know. I have to figure this out. So, I'm going to go and see if it helps. I'll let you know how it goes."

Carrie picked up the gossip magazine from the table by her grandmother's bed. She flipped through it trying to find an article she thought her grandmother would like. She finally settled on a story about George Clooney and read it out loud to her.

"Did you like that, Gram?" she asked when she finished reading. "I know you have a little crush on George. What is it you always said about him? Oh yeah. 'He's a really good-looking fella.' Remember saying that, Gram?"

Carrie laughed at the memory. She had a lot of memories of her grandmother. She spent the first seventeen years of her life living next door to her. Carrie loved her mom and they got along like most mothers and daughters. Sometimes fine and other times—well, other times not so fine. They went through a particularly rough time in their relationship when Carrie was in her teens. But no matter how things were going with her mother, Carrie loved going next door and visiting her grandmother. [Gram]

Her house always felt warm and inviting. The smell of something baking usually filled the air. Gram was free with her hugs and always had time for Carrie. She was famous in the neighborhood for her homemade pies and it wasn't unusual for her to be making one, or three, when Carrie would show up unannounced. Gram always seemed to have an extra piece of dough for her, and Carrie would roll it with her miniature rolling pin, working that piece of dough until it was smooth and flat. With Gram's help, she would place it in her little pie pan. After they filled the crusts with fruit and sugar and put them in the oven, Carrie got to turn the dial on the old white timer with the big red numbers.

Gram was more than a grandmother. She was a second mother and Carrie's best friend. Grandpa had died suddenly when Carrie was nine. It was a very rough time, but she spent more time with her grandmother to help out in any way she could. It brought them even closer together.

Carrie could talk to her grandmother about anything, and Gram in return, told her stories about what it was like when she was young, when you were supposed to conform and be like everyone else. Gram refused the cookie-cutter mold society wanted to force her into. She might have even been considered a rebel in her youth.

But now Carrie was doing all the talking, and she hoped her grandmother was listening.

CHAPTER TWO

Carrie leaned against the wall directly across from the door with number seventeen written in what looked like black permanent marker. The drab gray hallway reminded her of a basement. The dim light from a single light bulb did nothing to change that impression. The handwritten sign—just a piece of plain white paper taped to the door—announced that this was the room for the grief support group. Now that she was here she wasn't sure she wanted to go in. Everyone in that room had lost a loved one. She hadn't. Her grandmother was still alive. Did she have a right to be here? Was her grief premature? Was she dismissing her grandmother as dead before she really was? She stood, lifting her back from the wall, and smoothed down the front of her shirt. It wasn't fancy, but it was dressier than the T-shirts she often wore when she wasn't working. Carrie looked once again at the sign on the door as if it would tell her what to do. It didn't.

She was still standing there when a woman rounded the corner and almost ran into her.

"Oh my God. I'm so sorry," the woman said as she stopped a step short of Carrie. The woman was a couple of inches taller than Carrie's five foot five. Her dark brown hair had a bit of a wave to it and hung several inches below her shoulders. Carrie guessed her to be about the same age, maybe a little bit older.

Carrie's attention was drawn to her amber brown eyes. Ringed in a dark brown with flecks of gold, they could only be described as beautiful. Her soft features were accentuated by a summer tan that still lingered despite the fact that it was nearly fall. The hint of makeup she wore was just enough to highlight those soft features. The floral print blouse and black dress pants she wore gave her an understated elegant look.

Carrie took a sideways step. "No, my fault," she said.

The woman seemed to hesitate before speaking. "Are you here for the grief group?" She raised her eyebrows with the question, making those brown eyes seem even bigger and brighter, even with the bad lighting in the hallway.

Carrie cleared her throat. "Um, well, good question. I am, but I'm still deciding if I want to go in."

The woman ran her fingers through her hair, smoothing it down with what appeared to be some anxiety. The waves fell right back into place as the fingers released them. "I'm not sure I want to go in either, to tell you the truth. But I promised someone I would. So if it would help, we can sit together." A bit of a smile tugged at the corners of her mouth.

Having someone, even a stranger, to sit with might make it easier. "Okay," Carrie said. "I made it this far, I might as well go all the way."

The woman opened the door and gestured for Carrie to go in first. Carrie nodded her thanks and crossed the threshold. A group of people were scattered around the room that wasn't much brighter than the hallway they'd just left. Carrie wondered if this was done purposely to try to give the room a somber feel. If so, it was working. In the center of the room sat a dozen or so metal folding chairs arranged in a loose circle. A long table with a cheap yellow plastic tablecloth sat against one wall. It held several plates of cookies, cheese and crackers, and other goodies. A coffee maker with a full pot of coffee sat next to the food.

Carrie caught the eye of a tall man with a thick mustache and thin, greasy black hair. He had evidently watched them walk in. Tufts of equally black hair speckled with gray peeked out of the top of his tight-fitting faded T-shirt. His eyes traveled up the length of Carrie, pausing on her breasts before briefly looking at her face. Carrie was sure she saw him wink at her. She turned to her companion to see if she'd noticed his rude behavior. She hadn't. Her attention appeared to be on the plate of cookies on the end of the table.

A well dressed middle-aged man entered the room through a second doorway in the back. There was a cheerful air about him despite the lack of a smile on his face. He set a stack of napkins on the table and a box of Kleenex on one of the folding chairs. He surveyed the people in the room before speaking.

"Hello, can I get everyone's attention please? Everyone." The room grew quiet as the group turned toward the speaker. "All right. I think everyone is here now," he said. "If you would each like to take a seat we can get started." Everyone slowly made their way to the circle of chairs.

Carrie sat next to the woman she had met at the door. She ran her hands nervously over her jeans as if she were wiping off sweaty palms. Doubts crept back in and surrounded her like an unfriendly hug as she glanced around the room at the now seated group. She wasn't sure this was where she belonged. The feeling that she was betraying her grandmother overwhelmed her. Her eyes filled with tears, and she fought the urge to cry.

The leader spoke again. "I would like to welcome everyone here tonight." He passed the box of Kleenex around the circle. Carrie pulled out several of the thin sheets and wiped her eyes. "We'll start by going around the group and introducing ourselves and saying a little bit about why we're here. You can say whatever you're comfortable with or you can pass if you would rather do that for now." He cleared his throat. "I'll start." He told the group his name was Eric. He started working as a group facilitator after finding help with his own grieving process after losing his wife only four years into their marriage in a car accident, thirteen years ago. This was his fourth time leading a support group like this one. When he finished, he asked the young woman on his left to introduce herself.

Each person in turn took the floor and told their stories of sadness and the loss that brought them here. Each story was filled with emotion and pain, until the man with the thick mustache and greasy hair took the floor.

"Hey, everyone." He smiled, showing a mouth full of nicotine-yellowed teeth. "My name is Mike and my wife died four months ago and I have decided it's time to get over my grief and get out into the world again. I'm tired of being alone when I have so much to offer. So, I figured I got to get over this stuff if I am going to find the next Miss Right."

Was this guy for real? Carrie looked around the circle as he continued to talk. A few people looked a little shocked, but most looked like they were too absorbed in their own thoughts to notice. He went on and on about putting himself back into circulation, sounding more like a bad ad for a dating service than someone missing his spouse. After several minutes of his rambling, the leader cut him off.

"Thanks, Mike," Eric said and motioned for the next person to introduce themselves.

Carrie felt the heat rise to her face when it was her turn to speak. She couldn't put into words how she was grieving for her grandmother who was still alive. "I'm going to pass," she said without making eye contact with anyone. To her surprise, the woman she had met outside the room also passed.

"I think we'll stop here and take a fifteen-minute break," Eric said when the last person had introduced themselves. "Please feel free to help yourself to the snacks." He headed directly to the coffee.

Carrie leaned forward in her chair and rested her chin on her hands, her elbows resting on her thighs. The threat of tears had stopped, but she was still feeling out of place. She closed her eyes and took a deep breath as the rest of the group headed to the food. Someone sat in the now empty chair next to her and bumped her knee. She opened her eyes and expected to see the woman from the hallway but found herself looking into Mike's face instead. His beady eyes felt like they were boring into her, and she shifted uncomfortably in her chair.

"Hey," Mike said. Another wink. "I just wanted you to know that I noticed you and I'm a good listener if you want to talk about your being sad or anything. I'm really good at, umm, *listening*. If you get my drift."

Carrie couldn't believe her ears. "No, thank you." She shook her head. Whoa. Yuck.

"Don't be like that. I'm just offering my services to help in your time of need." He flashed her a grin that Carrie suspected was supposed to be seductive but was disgusting at best.

"Services?" she grimaced, sorry she asked as soon as the words were out of her mouth.

"Yeah, you know what I'm talking about."

Carrie wasn't rude by nature but didn't see a way out of this but to be blunt. "Well, I'm not interested."

"Oh, come on, baby, we could be good together. I just know it." If she didn't know any better, she would have sworn she was being punked. How could anyone be so—so—obnoxious?

"Really. Not. Interested," Carrie said a little more harshly than she intended. Mike left without another word. Carrie watched him strut over to the woman from the hallway and the animated conversation that followed. The woman took a step backward away from him, and he took a step forward. Unbelievable. *I should rescue her from that creep.*

Carrie forced herself to her feet and headed for Mike and the friendly brown-eyed woman. "Excuse me, Mike. I need to speak to umm…" Carrie realized she didn't know the woman's name. "…er, um, this beautiful lady here." *Oh my God, I can't believe I just said that.*

"Will you excuse me?" the beautiful lady said to Mike as Carrie pulled her away by the elbow. "Thank you so much. I couldn't seem to get that guy away from me," she said, as soon as they were out of earshot. A smile spread across her face. "I owe you one."

"I was actually thinking of leaving. I don't think this is the group for me," Carrie confessed. She shrugged.

"How about I buy you a cup of coffee somewhere? I don't feel much like staying either. My name is Hope by the way." She put out her hand. "Hope Garret."

"Carrie Martin." She shook the hand Hope extended. "I would love to go get coffee, or maybe a drink? I feel like I could use a gin and tonic about now. I think there is a quiet little bar just down the street. We could walk if that's okay with you."

"Sure, that would be great. Should we say something to Eric, or just leave?"

Carrie glanced over at Eric, engrossed in a conversation with two women. "I say we sneak out."

"Then let's do it," Hope said. She grabbed Carrie's hand and headed toward the door, dropping it as soon as the door closed behind them. They burst out laughing.

"Oh my God. That was intense," Carrie said. "Except for that Mike guy. He was just gross. You didn't have to leave with me. But I'm glad you did."

"I was happy to leave. I really didn't want to be here in the first place. Let's go find that bar."

The early evening air was unusually warm for mid September. The weather in Western New York could vary greatly in late summer, but the past week had been unusually sunny and warm. They made small talk as they walked the two blocks under the bright streetlights to the small bar on the corner of Monroe Avenue and Club Street.

Carrie held the heavy wooden door open for Hope. She blinked several times as they entered to let her eyes adjust to the darkness inside. A few booths with thick green cushions lined the wall to the right, and small tables with chairs were set around the center of the room. Shelves of alcohol surrounding a mirror sporting the name Budweiser in the familiar logo sat on the back wall behind the long bar. The place was empty except for two older guys playing pool in the corner and two younger men sitting at the bar drinking, a barstool separating them. Soft music drifted through the air, cut occasionally by the sound of billiard balls smacking into each other.

Carrie led the way to the stools at the far side of the bar, away from the two young men. "How's this?" she asked.

"This works." Hope set her small purse on the bar as she slid her body, seemingly effortlessly, onto the tall barstool.

Carrie climbed on the stool next to the wall, swiveled it toward Hope, and said, "I hope you don't mind I suggested a drink instead of coffee." She needed one to calm her nerves after feeling so out of place at the meeting and her encounter with creepy Mike.

"Not at all. I was just happy to get out of there. Although I did feel a little like a teenager skipping out of class." Hope smiled, revealing a row of almost perfect white teeth. One tooth leaned a little to the left, the imperfection only adding to her beauty.

"I know what you mean. I felt a little weird leaving like that, too. But going there in the first place was a bad idea."

The tall bartender appeared in front of them. He wiped his hands on a small towel tucked into his waistband and asked, "What can I get for you ladies?"

Hope looked at Carrie. "Gin and tonic, right?"

Carrie nodded, surprised Hope remembered the drink she had mentioned earlier.

Hope turned back to the bartender. "One gin and tonic and I'll have an, umm, I'll have a screwdriver, please." Hope looked momentarily flustered before she added in a low voice. "Hold the vodka."

The bartender smiled and leaned closer. "One gin and tonic and one virgin screwdriver, coming right up," he said in an equally low voice. Hope tilted her head and looked at Carrie, shrugging. "I don't really drink." She put her hand up. "Don't get me wrong, I have nothing against it. I just never developed a taste for alcohol."

"I'm so sorry. We should have gone for coffee like you suggested," Carrie said. She might have been a little too pushy suggesting a bar.

"No, no. You get your drink and I am perfectly happy with orange juice. Not a problem at all." She pulled a few bills from her purse and set it on the bar. "For both drinks," she said to the bartender.

"Thanks. Next round is on me," Carrie said.

"So, if you don't mind my asking, how come going to that meeting was a bad idea? I don't mean to be so blunt, but who died?"

"Hmm, well, I guess that's the problem. No one died. Yet." Carrie struggled to find the words to explain.

"I'm not sure I understand. Doesn't one usually go to a grief support group because someone died?" Hope's words were soft and kind.

"My grandmother is actually still alive, but she's been in a coma for almost three months. A vegetative state, the doctors call it. I visit a lot and talk to her, but she can't talk back, of course. I'm not even sure if she can hear what I am saying. I just miss her so much I thought it might be a good idea to go to a grief group to see if it would help."

"And why did you change your mind? Why did you want to leave?"

"Because I felt like I was writing my grandmother off as dead already. Like I was being disloyal to her. Does that make any sense?"

"Perfect sense," Hope said. The bartender set the drinks in front of them.

Carrie took a long swig. The liquid felt cool in her throat as it went down but warmed when it hit her belly.

"So, I assume you're close to your grandmother?" Hope asked.

"Really close. She lived next door and I was over there all the time when I was a kid. My grandparents had this big old farmhouse. It had like five bedrooms and only one teeny, tiny bathroom. But it had this huge kitchen that always smelled so good." Carrie watched the ice dance as she swirled the drink in her hand and memories filled her mind. "My grandmother always paid attention to me. She made me feel special." Carrie took another swallow of her drink. "She was—is—was…" Carrie shook her head. "Anyway, the woman knew how to bake. We were always making something delicious. She taught me what comfort food was. I can't eat a piece of pie or cake without thinking of her." Carrie paused for a beat, pushing the memories aside. "My grandmother may still be alive, but she isn't there anymore. I miss her. A lot. But I guess I'm not ready to grieve for her. I just couldn't face telling a room full of strangers that I missed my grandmother who's still alive. Especially when they were all talking about someone they lost." Carrie looked into Hope's eyes and saw a hint of sadness there. At first, she thought Hope was sympathizing with her. Then it hit her. "Oh my God. Here I am going on and on and you were there, too. You must have lost someone you love. I am so sorry."

"Oh, no, no. Don't be sorry. Yes. I was there, but only because I promised my sister I would go." She paused. "She thinks I'm in denial."

"Denial is the first stage of grief isn't it? Does your sister think you're stuck there?" Carrie had read all about the stages, trying to figure out her own feelings concerning her grandmother.

"It's not that I'm stuck there. It's that I'm not grieving at all. It's a really long story, but the bottom line is, my husband died after a three-year battle with cancer. I didn't, um, well, I didn't…"

Carrie sensed her discomfort. "It's okay. You don't have to tell me if you don't want to."

Hope searched Carrie's deep green eyes. Something in Carrie's face told her it was okay to go on. "I've never said these words out loud to anyone before." She hesitated and took a deep breath, trying to work up her courage to speak her truth. The truth she'd kept buried so deep inside her she had to take an imaginary pickaxe to dig it out. "I was going to leave my husband. I had actually prepared to go, but he told me he had cancer. So, I stayed." Hope swallowed down the lump in her throat. "I'd found an apartment for me and my son. Derrick was sixteen at the time. I was going to sign the lease the following day. My marriage hadn't been working for a long time and I felt like it was time to face that. Tom was diagnosed with colon cancer, and I decided to stay to help him through it. It ended up he didn't get better, and I stayed and took care of him until he died."

"Did he know you were going to leave him?" Carrie asked quietly.

"No. No one knew. I wasn't going to tell him until I had everything for my new life worked out." Hope sighed. It felt good to be sharing. It somehow relieved some of the burden that had been weighing her down. "I didn't want him to try to talk me out of it. I wanted to be ready to go when I told him. And I never told anyone else out of respect for Tom. I didn't think it was fair to tell someone else before I told him. So I hadn't said anything to anyone. He wasn't a bad guy or even a bad husband. He just wasn't the person I wanted to come home to every day.

I'm not sure he ever was. So, when he died my primary feeling was guilt." A guilt she still held a part of. A guilt she feared would never go away.

"Guilty because you were going to leave him?" Carrie asked.

"No." The rest was even harder to say. What would this woman think of her when she learned the truth? "I felt guilty because I felt relieved when he died. I know that sounds terrible. But it's true." She couldn't believe she was saying this out loud.

"I'm so sorry to burden you with all this. You don't even know me, yet you are kind enough to listen to me ramble on."

"I feel privileged you feel comfortable enough to tell me," Carrie said. "Sometimes the best person to tell your secrets to is a complete stranger." She drained the rest of her drink and held up her empty glass to get the bartender's attention. "I'll get a virgin screwdriver," she said to the bartender. "And get my friend here a refill, too. Thanks."

"You don't have to stop drinking because of me."

"One is my limit when I am driving," Carrie answered. "Go on," she said to Hope.

Hope still couldn't believe she was admitting such personal details to someone she didn't really know. But Carrie made it easy. She seemed to be listening without judgment. "I'm pretty sure that group isn't going to help me with the guilt. It's not that I wanted him to die, because I didn't. I didn't want my son to be without his father for one thing. I never wanted that. I fully expected to stay with him until he got better." Hope pushed away the memory of her husband in his final days. So weak. So frail. So needy. "Tom would be okay for a while, and I would think he would get better and live. Then he would take a turn for the worse, and I was sure he was going to die, and I would set my mind to accepting it. Then he would get better again and the cycle would repeat. My emotions were like a damn yo-yo. It was so draining. Finally, he took a turn for the worse and just got sicker and sicker, and it got harder and harder to take care of him. But I did. I took care of him until the end."

"You're a very special person to do that for him."

Hope studied Carrie's face for a moment. Her green eyes held a sincerity that made Hope feel safe.

"I certainly don't feel special. I did what anyone would do."

"I disagree. I think you did much more than most people would have done. I don't think you have anything to feel guilty about, Hope." Carrie patted Hope's hand. The contact was warm and appreciated. It struck Hope how long it had been since she'd had human contact of *any* kind. She'd missed it.

The bartender set two glasses of orange juice in front of them as they sat in comfortable quiet for several long moments. Carrie broke the silence. "So you have a son?"

Hope's pride swelled. "Yes, Derrick's nineteen now. He goes to college in Buffalo. Probably going to go into business like his father. He's a good kid. I'm very proud of him."

"It shows." Carrie tucked a strand of dark blond hair behind her ear.

"He's the kind of kid who never causes too much trouble, you know. Well, if we don't count the three years he was in middle school and his first two years of high school." Hope let out a small laugh. "But I hear that happens a lot. Luckily, he seemed to come to his senses when he was a junior. I'm pretty sure I heard an actual pop one day when his head came out of his ass. Not that it doesn't go back in every once in a while."

Carrie, who had just taken a drink of her juice, sputtered, mouth full of liquid. She managed to swallow it without spewing it across the bar and wiped a drip that escaped down her chin.

"Sorry," Hope said, amused. "Didn't mean to make you choke." She let out her own wave of laughter.

Carrie smiled at her. "Yeah, I can tell by your laugh just how sorry you are." She shook her head.

"I really am sorry," Hope said when she finally got the laughing under control. "Oh my God, I haven't laughed like that in a long time."

"You should do it more often," Carrie told her. "It looks good on you."

"Thanks," Hope said. "Okay, enough about me. Let's talk about you. Married? Boyfriend? Kids?"

The bartender set a fresh bowl of pretzels in front of them. Hope reached for a handful and pushed the bowl closer to Carrie.

Carrie shook her head at the silent offer. "None of the above."

"Never?" Hope asked between bites.

"Well, I had boyfriends when I was younger, if that's what you are asking. And no current boyfriend. I did however break up with my last girlfriend a little over three years ago. Been single since then."

Girlfriend, huh? Okay. She hadn't pegged Carrie as being a lesbian. Not that it mattered. "How come someone as stunning as you doesn't have someone special in your life?" Hope said. "Sorry. That didn't sound quite right." But Carrie was stunning. Dark blond hair that hung just below her shoulders, deep green eyes and the slightest cleft in her chin added up to a very attractive woman. Hope imagined there would be a lot of people, men and women, who would be vying for her attention.

"Thanks for the compliment." She shrugged. "I just can't seem to meet a woman who holds my interest for more than a couple of dates, and some for not even that long. My love life is a sad, sad thing." She shook her head but grinned at Hope. "It's okay. It gets lonely sometimes, but I'm happy with my life for the most part. I certainly don't need someone to *make* me happy." Carrie seemed to think for a moment. Her face betrayed her regret at her choice of words. "I'm sorry," she said. "That was insensitive of me, considering everything you have been through."

"Stop. I didn't take it personally. I don't want you to have to watch every word you say."

"Okay, thanks."

"So, what do you do for a living?" Hope asked.

"I'm a logistics manager at the Freddrick's Company. In charge of the warehouse inventory, transportation, some customer service. I know it sounds glamorous, but not so much."

"Are you trying to tell me you don't get to wear an evening gown to work with three-inch heels and a tiara every day?"

"Oh, well, yeah I do. So, if you count that, then I guess it is pretty darn glamorous," Carrie laughed at her own joke. Hope found it endearing.

"Doesn't your evening gown get dirty in the warehouse?"

"Not really. There are three guys whose only job is to carry me around and keep me away from the dirt."

"Sounds like a dream job." Hope was enjoying the evening much more than she ever thought she would when she begrudgingly got ready for the grief support group.

"Actually, it is a pretty good job. I've been with the company for twelve years. The benefits are good, and I've got about a million days of vacation time built up."

"A million, huh? That's a lot. Do you get that every year?" Hope sipped her drink and relaxed into the conversation.

"No, I get four weeks a year because I've been there so long, but I haven't taken much of it, so it just accumulates."

"You don't ever take vacations?"

"Not usually. I don't feel like going anywhere alone. I do too much alone. I have friends, but most of them have significant others or families. I used to take my grandmother to North Carolina every year to visit my brother, but it got hard for her to travel, so we haven't done it in a while."

"What do you do when you aren't working or visiting your grandmother?" Hope asked.

"I paint," Carrie said. "I love creating art."

Hope leaned forward. "What kind of painting?"

"I oil paint—still lifes mostly, but I occasionally do portraits or figure painting. In fact, I have been working on a series of rough sketches for a show in New York City in December. I just need to find a model…" She stopped talking and looked at Hope.

Hope raised her eyebrows waiting for Carrie to finish. "What?"

Carrie cleared her throat. "Um, I was saying I need a model to use for a set of paintings for this show in New York City, and I was just deciding if I had enough nerve to ask you if you would consider posing for me."

"And what did you decide? Do you have enough nerve?" Hope teased her.

"No, probably not. I don't want you to think I am some sort of weirdo asking you to pose for me when you don't even know me."

"Who says I don't already think you're a weirdo?" Hope fought the urge to laugh.

"Well, in that case what do I have to lose? Would you consider posing for me? I would pay you, of course. You wouldn't get rich, but I could give you something for your time."

Hope was quiet as she gave it a moment of serious consideration.

"Have you ever modeled before? I mean, have you ever done modeling for art, for an artist." Carrie seemed to be stumbling over her words. It was charming.

"Actually, I did some modeling for art classes in college, but I was young and beautiful then." She smiled. "Now I'm old and wrinkly with stretch marks. I'm not sure I would be what you're looking for."

Carrie smiled back. "You are very far from old and wrinkly, and a few stretch marks won't hold me back."

"Are we talking about posing in the nude?" Hope realized that should have been her first question.

"Actually, we are talking about posing with a narrow strip of cloth draped around you covering your…" Carrie hesitated, "… female parts. So, I guess the answer would be yes and no. You would need to be nude under the material, but it would cover your womanly parts, so to speak. I'm sorry, this is probably pretty weird, having a stranger ask you this."

"No, not at all. Strangers ask me to get naked all the time, and some are even willing to pay me for it." Hope popped another pretzel in her mouth.

"You're just a smart-ass, aren't you?"

"Pretty much." Hope grinned. "But I will consider posing for you. How's that?"

"That would be great. Think about it and let me know." Carrie pulled her phone from her pocket, opened it to new contacts, and slid it across the bar to Hope. Hope typed her number in and slid it back.

It took Carrie only a few seconds to send a quick text. "There you go. Now you have my number."

Hope smiled when she heard the text tone from her phone in her purse. She didn't really need the extra money. Tom had left her very comfortable. But maybe she could pose *and* make a new friend. And if there was one thing in her life she needed right now it was a friend.

CHAPTER THREE

Hope put the bottle of salad dressing on the table and sat across from her sister. Marcy's short hair no longer matched Hope's chestnut brown. Hope wasn't crazy about the new copper red color that now graced her head. Marcy's eyes were every bit as brown as Hope's but lacked the flecks of gold. As usual, she was dressed impeccably in a peach shirt and a black pleated skirt that hugged her small hips and butt perfectly. A thin black belt with a silver buckle and a peach silk scarf around her neck completed the look.

Hope's dining room was elegant but comfortable. An understated chandelier hung over the solid maple dining table surrounded by six chairs. A matching china cabinet stood at attention against the far wall.

Hope placed a generous amount of salad on her plate and poured blue cheese dressing over it. She accepted the slice of Italian bread from Marcy without making eye contact. She kept her attention on her food until Marcy spoke.

"So, you aren't going to tell me how it went at the grief group last night?" Marcy asked her.

Hope took a bite of the bread and chewed it slowly as she formulated her answer. "It was fine." The less words the better. A change of subject would be good here. "How are the kids?"

"What aren't you telling me?" Marcy obviously didn't fall for her tactic. "You did go, didn't you? Hope, you promised me you would go to that group." The sharp edge to her voice made Hope cringe.

"Yes, Marcy." She looked her in the eye. There was no getting around this conversation. She should have just told Marcy she was busy when she invited herself over for lunch. "I went," she said. Maybe a little too loudly. She looked down at her plate again. "I just didn't stay."

Hope closed her eyes and rubbed her temples, dreading Marcy's response. Silence. Long. Silence. Hope looked at her and recognized that look of disappointment. She had seen it on her mother's face often enough. She wondered if it would be worth the effort to try to explain.

"Marcy," she started. "It just didn't feel right. I went, but it didn't seem like I fit with the people there. It wasn't where I needed to be." She knew how lame it must have sounded. She pushed her plate forward. Her appetite had disappeared.

"Hope." Marcy had a way of saying her name and making it sound like a reprimand. "You promised me you would go. Did I need to make you promise me you would stay?" She put her fork down and folded her hands in front of her, waiting for an answer.

Hope was determined not to let her big sister treat her like a child. She was thirty-seven years old, not six. She was damn well old enough to leave a group she didn't feel comfortable in. She took a deep breath before speaking. Making eye contact, she said, "Marcy, I know you're just trying to help me. You think I need to share my grief with other people. But this type of group is *really* not what I need." She closed her eyes for a moment to gain her composure. When she opened them again, she saw the disappointment in Marcy's eyes had been replaced with concern. "The night was not a total loss. I met a woman there. Carrie. We talked after we left the meeting. We talked for a long time. She seemed to understand what I'm going through, and she listened to me. Really listened. I think talking to her helped. So, please don't think I am not getting help going through this."

"You're telling me you spent the evening spilling your guts to a total stranger and now you feel better? Why couldn't you stay in the group and get some real help? I care about you, Hope. I want you to heal so you can go on with your life." She paused briefly. "You haven't grieved at all and I think that's just not normal. I don't understand how talking to some woman you don't even know could make you feel better."

"But I *did* feel better after talking to her. Why do you object to my speaking about this to one stranger, but you want me to tell my story to a roomful of strangers?" She did her best to explain but had the feeling it was falling on deaf ears. "Isn't that the point—to have someone I can share this with, who can share her story with me? And in the end we both feel better." She shook her head in frustration. *Fricken' stop already.*

"Pass me the salad dressing," Marcy demanded, startling Hope with the sudden change in topic and the harsh tone. She handed the bottle to her. Marcy drowned her salad in the chunky ooze, and began cutting the lettuce into little pieces, with more force than seemed necessary. She stabbed a chunk of lettuce and brought it to her mouth. She held it there as she stared at Hope. Hope could almost feel her eyes burning holes into her. Several drops of dressing fell from her fork back onto her plate. Finally, Marcy pushed the lettuce into her mouth and chewed. Slowly. She pointed her fork at Hope. "I'm not sure what to say to convince you that you are making a huge mistake. I think you need help dealing with everything and I don't think meeting some stranger and having an in-depth discussion is going to do it. But I guess it could be worse. I guess you could have told me you met a man at the meeting and decided to start dating already."

Hope tried to suppress a laugh, to no avail. It came bubbling out. "That is something you definitely don't have to worry about. I am in no rush to start dating any men." She shook her head and laughed again. "Can we just call a truce here? I don't want to fight with you. I know you're trying to help. But I really don't think going to a support group is right for me. Let's just sit here and play nice and enjoy lunch. Can we do that?" She tilted her head. "Please?"

Marcy let out a cross between a groan and a huff. She looked at Hope for several seconds longer. "Okay, I'll drop it for now, but we are going to talk about this again. You need to move on with your life and your denying there is a problem doesn't make the problem go away. I know what I'm talking about, Hope. You should be listening to me."

Hope knew Marcy wouldn't let it go completely and at some point, they would revisit the subject. She hoped it wasn't too soon. It would give her time to be better prepared the next time.

CHAPTER FOUR

Carrie's mother rearranged the knick-knacks on the small table next to Gram's bed for the third time. Carrie watched in silence. Her endless chatter was giving Carrie a headache. It was so much better when she was alone during these visits with her grandmother.

"I brought more of these cute little collie figurines, Mom," her mother said directly to Gram. "I know when you wake up you are really going to love them." She held one in front of Gram's closed eyes and then held it up for Carrie to see. Carrie nodded. "I also took your car in for an oil change yesterday. I know you're always..." Carrie tuned out her mother's voice. Her mind wandered to the previous evening and meeting Hope. Her idea about joining a support group was misguided, but it turned out well if it meant she made a new friend. And Hope would be the perfect model for her project. Carrie hoped she would seriously consider it.

Her mother continued to talk as she ran her hand over her jet-black hair, no visible gray, courtesy of Miss Clairol. She refused to show her age and spent far too much money on magic creams and lotions in Carrie's opinion. Her grandmother had aged naturally and gracefully and beautifully, a much better way to grow old.

Carrie absently rubbed the back of her neck trying to release the tension that was building there.

"…so, what do you think about that? Carrie?" The sound of her name brought her out of her thoughts.

"What did you say, Mom?" she asked.

"I swear I get about as much of a response out of you as I get out of your grandmother here." She didn't try to hide her annoyance. "I asked you what you thought of this blanket." She held up the corner of the blanket covering the bed. It was a standard tan cotton weave blanket used by the nursing home.

"Do you think your grandmother likes this one, or should I bring her one from her house?"

Carrie sighed. "Which would *you* like better?"

"I like the one from her house and I think she would like it better, too. I am going to stop over there tomorrow and get it for her. How about that green one she has over the back of the couch? Don't you think that would be good? Or should I get her the one that's on her bed?"

Carrie nodded absently and picked up the current copy of *People* magazine she'd brought with her.

"Well, which one do you think would be better?" Her mother wasn't going to stop until she answered.

"The one from the couch would be fine."

"All righty then. I'll pick it up on my way home so I can wash it before I bring it here. I think it'll really cheer this room up."

Carrie thumbed through the magazine and looked for an interesting article to read to her grandmother. She knew her mother would be leaving soon. She never stayed long and she never stopped moving the whole time she was there. Carrie wanted alone time with her grandmother, so she would just wait her mother out. She didn't have to wait long.

"I have to get going," her mother said, offering no explanation.

She gave Carrie a hug and kissed Gram on the cheek. "Bye, Mother. I'll see you in a few days. Try to get some rest now." She patted Gram's hand. "Bye, Carrie," she said with a wave as she walked out the door.

"Bye, Mom," Carrie said, but her mother was already gone.

"Oh, Gram, I hope Mom didn't make you too crazy. Wish I could say the same for me. I know she means well. I guess she is just having her own problems handling all this. I think you've got the easy part, Gram, 'cause it's really hard for the rest of us. Anyway, I wanted to tell you about that support group I went to." Carrie pulled her chair closer to her grandmother. "Gram, I couldn't stay at it. Going wasn't a good idea. It wasn't what I needed, at least not right now. But I did manage to meet a new friend. You would like her. Her name is Hope and she was very nice. I really liked talking to her, and I think it helped me. So, the evening wasn't a total waste."

Carrie leaned back in her chair and smoothed out the magazine in her lap. She let out a long sigh and once again looked for an article to read to her grandmother. Nothing caught her eye so she put the magazine aside. She ran her hands over her jeans.

"I don't know what is wrong with me today," she said as much to herself as she did to her grandmother. "I guess I'm feeling a little lonely. I've felt lonely plenty of times before, but I could always call you, and just hearing your voice would always make me feel better. I miss that."

She walked to the window and looked out at the dull September sky. A total contrast to the past several days. The feelings of loneliness crept in more on the days like this.

Her thoughts once again went to the woman she had met the evening before. Carrie was sure they would become real friends. It had been a long time since she'd met someone she felt she clicked with, especially so soon. Carrie had friends, but she was picky about whom she spent her time with. She didn't have any desire to hang out with people just to have something to do. Between work, art, and now her regular visits with her grandmother, she had plenty to keep her busy.

There was something almost familiar about Hope, but Carrie was certain they had never met before. Maybe they met in another life. Carrie laughed to herself. She wasn't sure she believed such things. There was something definitely different about Hope that set her apart from her other friends. Whatever it was, it drew Carrie's attention.

❖

Carrie threw the mail on the kitchen table and opened the refrigerator, peering in. "I need to go grocery shopping," she said out loud. She checked the date on the packaged lunchmeat before deciding to make herself a sandwich for dinner. She grabbed the mayo, cheese, and a bottle of beer, and did a balancing act that would make any circus performer proud. She popped a hip against the fridge door to close it.

With her feet propped up on the coffee table and her plate on her lap, she sat on the couch and watched the evening news. The Hollywood gossip shows were beginning as she finished. Before the accident, her grandmother would have been glued to the television. She loved to keep track of the celebrity news.

Carrie took her plate and empty beer bottle to the kitchen and went to her bedroom to change her clothes. She emerged wearing an old T-shirt and a pair of well-worn, paint-stained jeans and continued on into her art studio.

"Alexa." She paused waiting for that familiar tone. "Play my painting play list." The room filled with the soft sounds of female voices, singing a variety of songs from the last three decades.

The converted spare bedroom was filled with a drawing table, a large easel, and a variety of art supplies. An old wooden table sat along one wall. Carrie had felt like she'd found a treasure when she spotted it at the local flea market two years ago. She ran her hand over the stressed wood, loving every scratch, dent, and imperfection. It was truly a table with character and history.

Carrie twisted the knob on the floor lamp. A cascade of light appeared and illuminated the still life setup Carrie had arranged the day before. She made a few small adjustments to the apples that sat on the old wooden cutting board and moved the paring knife so the blade caught the gleam of the light. She stood back and examined her arrangement. Satisfied, she donned her painting apron and sat on the stool in front of her easel. She stared at the still life setup for a full minute before bringing her attention to the blank canvas in front of her. She searched through her plastic bin of oil paints until she found the two colors she sought. She put a large dab of burnt sienna onto her palette and used odorless paint thinner to reduce the paint to a watery consistency. Carrie chose a wide brush and dipped it into the reddish-brown mixture. She dragged the brush across the white canvas, leaving a streak of color in its tracks. She continued working until color filled the whole canvas, then added more brush strokes in alternating directions.

After adding a generous dollop of burnt umber to her palette, she mixed the darker paint into the thin mixture. She switched to a smaller brush and loosely applied the paint to select areas, alternating with a small rag to remove paint to add highlights. Slowly, the rough underpainting of the still life began to emerge as her brush danced over the canvas.

It took only minutes for Carrie to get into the rhythm of painting and let her mind and body relax. Random thoughts came and went, most unnoticed. When an image of Hope waltzed into Carrie's mind, she did notice. Her paint brush stilled as she let the image fill her thoughts. I should call her, Carrie thought. She had thoroughly enjoyed talking to her two nights before and believed they could become friends. She also wanted to pursue the idea of using Hope as a model for her figure paintings. She was a beautiful woman, and beauty often inspired her artistic ideas, whether it was the simple beauty of a fresh apple or the intricate beauty of a woman.

Almost two hours later, Carrie squinted at the canvas in front of her. Satisfied with the values and basic forms, she stretched her arms above her head and twisted her back from side to side to work out the kinks that had settled in.

With her brushes cleaned and put away, Carrie turned off the music and lights and left the room. She lived alone, but closed the door anyway, as if protecting her art sanctuary from the rest of the house and the rest of the world.

Carrie checked the time on the grandfather clock in the hallway as she passed through to her bedroom. Eight o'clock. Not too late to make a phone call. She sat on the edge of her bed and stared at Hope's phone number for several seconds before hitting it, not sure why she was hesitating. It rang several times and Carrie was sure it was going to go to voice mail when she heard a breathless Hope say, "Hello?"

"Hey. It's Carrie—from the other night. I didn't catch you at a bad time did I?"

"Not at all, I was just reading. I forgot my cell phone upstairs and had to run to get it."

"Sorry about that."

"Stop. I'm glad you called, and now that I had to run up the stairs I have my exercise in for the day. So it's a win-win situation for me. How are you doing?"

"All right. Went to visit my grandmother for a little while today after work and then came home and painted."

"What did you paint?" Hope asked.

"The underpainting for a still life. I start out with two colors and just work on getting the shapes and values right. It doesn't look like much at the moment."

"I would love to see your work sometime. Do you paint often?"

"Usually two or three times a week. I think I would go crazy if I couldn't. It's like meditation for me. It is a great stress reliever," Carrie said. "How's your week going?"

Hope let out an audible sigh.

"That good, huh?" Carrie asked.

"No, for the most part it's been fine. Meeting you was definitely the highlight." Carrie could hear the smile in Hope's voice. "My sister on the other hand was a different story."

"Why is that?"

"She really lit into me about leaving that meeting."

"She was the reason you went in the first place, right?" Carrie leaned back on the bed and rested her head on the pillow.

"Yeah, she badgered me until I agreed to go, and she was not too pleased I left. I tried to explain I got more out of talking to you than I would have gotten out of the meeting."

"I feel the same." Carrie was glad she had decided to make the call. "It truly helped, and I wanted to say thank you for that."

"You're very welcome."

"I was wondering if you would like to come over this weekend. I could make us dinner, and we could talk about having you pose for my paintings if you are at all interested. And you can see my work."

"My son is coming home from college this weekend, but he'll be heading back Sunday afternoon. We could do Sunday evening if that works for you."

"That would be great. Any food restrictions I should know about? Anything in particular you like or don't like?" Carrie asked.

Hope paused before responding. "I am not crazy about anything hot, like hot sauce or hot peppers. Umm, and I don't like peas. But just about anything else would be fine."

"How about Italian?"

"I love Italian. I'm half Italian you know. The half my mouth and stomach are in, so Italian food makes me very happy." Hope let out a quiet laugh.

"Happy is good. Italian it is then. Does six o'clock work?"

"That would be fine."

"I'll text you the address as soon as we hang up."

"Perfect."

They talked for another thirty minutes, like they were old friends. Carrie was in a very good mood by the time she hung up the phone and typed out her address in the text box and hit *send*.

CHAPTER FIVE

Hope wrapped the cord around the vacuum cleaner and put it into the laundry room closet. She had spent half the day cleaning the house anticipating Derrick's arrival. Not that it was really messy, but it definitely had been a little neglected lately.

Her mood brightened as memories flooded in. It wasn't that long ago she was vacuuming up cookie crumbs or some other mess Derrick had made. She found it hard to believe he was nineteen years old and a sophomore in college now. Sometimes it felt like she was barely older than that herself. But it had been eighteen years since Hope was his age. That was the year her life took a major turn, a turn she never would have predicted. She added a husband and a baby to her life. She dropped out of college after only one semester to have Derrick, while Tom stayed in school and finished his last two years, earning a bachelor's degree in business. Both Tom and Hope had worked part-time, struggling to afford baby food and diapers. Looking back now, she wasn't sure how they did it, but they somehow managed.

Funny how things worked out in life. Well, not really funny. She spent eighteen years in a marriage to a man she didn't love because she got pregnant with a child she did love. And how did a thing like that happen? How did a good girl in her first year of college, technically still a virgin—*I think technically a virgin*—get pregnant by someone she didn't love? One word summed it up. Fear. She shook her head to dislodge the memories. There was still plenty she wanted to get done before her son arrived.

The last load of bed sheets was still warm from the dryer as she piled them into the laundry basket. Derrick's voice cut through the silence. "Mom? Are you home? I'm here. Mom?"

He always was an impatient kid. Hope called out, "I'm in the laundry room. Be right there." Derrick was already sitting at the kitchen table eating cookies when Hope walked into the kitchen and gave him a hug from behind.

"Hi," an unfamiliar voice off to her left said. She turned and looked into the bright blue eyes of a young woman, petite and cute with light brown hair that hung down her back. She looked to be about Derrick's age.

"Umm, hi," Hope said to the stranger. She smacked Derrick on the arm. "An introduction would be nice here, Derrick. Where were you raised? In a barn?"

Without waiting for a response, Hope offered her hand to the young woman. "Hi, I'm Hope. I'm Derrick's mother. I tried to raise him right, but apparently he has no manners."

The young woman shook her hand. "I'm Erin. I'm sure Derrick's rude behavior doesn't reflect poorly on you." She smiled warmly.

Derrick swallowed a mouthful of cookies. "Mom, Erin." He waved his hand in the air. "Erin, Mom. Erin's my girlfriend. I was going to introduce you, but I had food in my mouth. You always told me not to talk with my mouth full."

"Nice to meet you, Erin," Hope said, surprised not only that Erin was here, but that Derrick had failed to even mention he had a girlfriend. "How long have you two been together?"

"Mom," Derrick said. "I'll fill you in at dinner. Are we still going to Super Steak? You'll love it, Erin. Stupid name but great food."

Hope roughed up Derrick's dark curly hair. He had gotten his brown eyes from her, but that hair was definitely from his father. "Yes, we're still going."

"Mom," Derrick complained. "It took me an hour to get my hair just right and you messed it up."

"Oh, so sorry, poor baby." She roughed it up again. Both Derrick and Hope laughed as he ducked from under her hands. "Better get up to your room and get all freshened up if you expect me to take you out in public, kiddo. You can show Erin the guest room and bathroom."

"Erin can just sleep in my room with me," Derrick said, not looking at her.

"Um, I'm thinking no, she can sleep in the guest room." Hope kept her voice calm and even. She knew this wouldn't escalate to an argument, and although he might push a little, Derrick would respect her wishes. She also knew he would do his best to get his way before giving in.

"Come on, Mom. Erin's twenty and I'm almost twenty. We're old enough to sleep in the same bed if we want to."

"You have eight months before you're twenty. And besides that's not any sort of magic number that you get to do whatever you want to in my house. So Erin is more than welcome here and she will have a lovely night's sleep in the guest room." Hope paused to let it sink in. She had made her point, careful not to belittle her son in front of his girlfriend. "Now, would you like to show Erin the room or would you like me to?"

"I'll do it," Derrick said. "Come on, Erin. I'll show you *your* room." Derrick gave a sheepish grin. He took Erin's hand and headed in the direction of the stairs.

"Hey!" Hope called after him. "Make sure you comb your hair while you're up there. It's a mess." She shook her head and smiled to herself.

❖

The waiter refilled Hope's water glass. "Is there anything else I can get for anyone?" he asked.

"Thank you, no. I think we're all set," Hope told him. She cut into her steak. "What are you majoring in, Erin?" Hope asked, turning her attention to Derrick's new girlfriend.

"Education," she answered. "I want to be an elementary school teacher."

"That's wonderful. I always thought Derrick would make a great teacher. He's really good with kids."

Erin nodded. "He probably would. But he also seems to have a good head for business."

"Yes, he does. He got that from his father. And how long have the two of you been together?" Hope couldn't help herself. She had never heard Derrick mention Erin's name before and she wanted all the details.

"Four months. We were both taking summer classes," Derrick said through a mouth full of food. "Erin picked me up in a bar." He laughed.

Erin swatted his arm. "I did not."

"I'm really hoping you didn't meet in a bar considering you're both too young to be drinking." She looked first at Derrick and then at Erin. She didn't really want to know the answer. She had given Derrick enough lectures on underage drinking, amongst other things and she was sure that another one now wouldn't make any difference.

"We met at a party off campus, Mrs. Garret, and I certainly didn't pick Derrick up. He came over and started talking to me. I had no interest in him at first. I mean, look at him." Erin grinned. "He has a face only a mother could love." She giggled.

I like this girl. She's a good match for Derrick and his off-beat sense of humor.

"Hey," Derrick said.

"Oh, baby, I'm just teasing, ya." Erin put her hand over his.

Derrick grinned. "I asked Erin to go out for burgers the next night and we have been together since. I'm starting to think she likes me."

"Yeah, I like him," Erin said.

Hope had no doubts they liked each other. "Where are you from, Erin?"

"Near Buffalo."

"So, do you live at home or on campus?" Hope scooped up a forkful of carrots.

"On campus. I think my parents like it better that way." She laughed.

"I like it better that way." Derrick kissed her on the cheek causing a blush to creep up her neck.

Hope continued with her list of questions, careful not to overwhelm them or overstep. Erin filled her in on her short history with Derrick and some interesting stories about college life.

"Tell me some of the embarrassing stories from Derrick's childhood, Mrs. Garret," Erin said with a smile once Hope ran out of questions. "I'm sure he was a goofy kid, seeing he's such a goofy guy now."

"Hey," Derrick said.

Oh yeah, I like her. "Call me Hope. Mrs. Garret sounds so formal—and old." Hope tapped a finger against her chin. "Hmm, let's see. Embarrassing stories about Derrick. There are so many." Hope thought about it for a moment. "Oh, I know. There was this one time when Derrick was three and we all went camping—"

"Mom," Derrick said, "not that story."

"Yes," Erin said. "Let's start with that story."

Hope not only continued the story, she told several more. Derrick objected to each one but seemed to eat up the attention.

"Go ahead and order dessert," Hope said to Erin after they had finished their meals. "I know Derrick will." Hope looked over the dessert menu. "I think I'll have a little something, too."

Derrick didn't disappoint, ordering the most decadent dessert on the menu. Hope opted for something light, still full from her meal. Her thoughts turned to Sunday and the dinner Carrie promised to make for her. She was sure it would put the meal she had just eaten to shame.

CHAPTER SIX

D inner was in the oven and the house was straightened up. Carrie looked at herself in the bathroom mirror for the third time. She wanted to look her best when Hope arrived. She was starting to second-guess her choice of a cable-knit sweater over a button-down blouse. She shrugged at her reflection in the mirror. If she got too warm, she could always shed it without too much trouble. She took a large sip of mouthwash from a Dixie cup, silently counted to thirty, and spit it out. She let out an audible "ahh" as the liquid first burned and then cooled her mouth. A quick glance at the clock told her she still had twenty minutes to spare as she headed to her art studio.

She was thumbing through a stack of drawings when the doorbell rang. Hope was a few minutes early.

"I brought wine," Hope said as soon as Carrie opened the door. "Hi." She handed the bottle of red to her. "I hope this goes with Italian."

"Hi there." Carrie took a step back to let Hope pass. "I thought you didn't drink."

"I don't, but I didn't want to come empty-handed. Is red all right?"

"You didn't have to bring anything. But that was very sweet of you. Yes, red is great, and this is a very good wine," Carrie said, reading the label. Impressive.

Carrie took Hope's coat and hung it on the hook behind the door. Hope looked nice in a pink button-down shirt that was tucked neatly into her dark denim jeans. "I love that shirt," Carrie said.

"Thanks. It's new. I don't usually wear pink, but I liked this shade."

"Very nice. Come on in. Can I interest you in a glass of red wine?" Carrie asked with a smile, holding up the bottle.

Hope laughed. "No, but a glass of water would be great."

"Of course. Would you like ice and lemon?"

"Sure," Hope answered.

"Make yourself comfortable," Carrie told her, waving toward the living room. "There are appetizers on the coffee table. Help yourself. Be right back."

Carrie filled two glasses with ice and filtered water. She tossed in a lemon slice and returned to find Hope viewing one of her framed oil paintings. It was one of Carrie's favorites, her grandmother sitting in a rocking chair with her beloved collie, Duchess, by her side. Her gray hair hinted at her age, but her eyes still held the wonder of youth.

"Your grandmother?" Hope asked. She took the glass of water Carrie offered her. "Thanks."

"Yeah," Carrie answered. "I did it a few years ago."

"It's beautiful. You're very talented."

"Thank you. I have some figure drawings in my studio I wanted to show you, too. They're really rough, but it will give you an idea of what I have in mind." She paused. "That is *if* you decide to pose for me." Carrie really hoped she would. She was also looking forward to getting to know Hope better and the possibility of having a new friend. She had let many of her friends go by the wayside, between work, painting, and now spending so much time with her grandmother she hadn't made the time for them. She knew now that was a mistake. One she didn't plan on making again. "We can take a look at them after we eat. Supper is in the oven now."

"It smells wonderful."

"Sit." Carrie motioned to the couch and sat on a loveseat across from her. "Help yourself to some cheese puffs. It's my grandmother's recipe." Carrie nudged the plate closer to Hope. "How did the visit with your son go?"

"It was nice. He surprised me by bringing home a new girlfriend." She stuffed a cheese puff in her mouth. "Mmm, this is so good."

"So, you didn't know he had a girlfriend, or you didn't know he was bringing her?"

"I didn't know about her at all. He changes girlfriends as often as I change my underwear—and I do that at least every week."

Carrie laughed.

"He doesn't usually bring *anyone* home with him." She seemed to think about it for a second. "In fact, I think this is the first one. He would bring girls around when he was in high school but hasn't brought one home from college before."

"Was that okay with you? That he brought her?"

"It was fine. She seems like a nice girl. I like her. I wouldn't mind him hanging on to this one for a while." Hope helped herself to another cheese puff. "Derrick has a really offbeat sense of humor, and she seems like she can keep up with him just fine."

"Oh, I wonder where he gets that from," Carrie said with a grin. "That's good. Humor is important." And Hope seemed to have a great sense of humor. Yes, Carrie thought, I really like her—and her humor.

❖

The lasagna was delicious. Hope took another bite before letting Carrie know just how good it was. "Is this your grandmother's recipe, too?" She cut into her food and watched a piece of cheese ooze out onto her plate.

"No, I got it online." Carrie sipped her wine. "My grandmother is—was—is—more of a baker than a cook." She hesitated. "It sounds stupid to talk about her in the past tense when she is still around."

Hope's heart hurt for her. "How is she doing?"

"The same. It really doesn't look like she is ever going to wake up. But there's a piece of me still holding out hope. You know what I mean?"

"I know exactly what you mean." Hope nodded.

"I know it's dumb. I mean I know the reality of the situation. But I can't seem to help it. My mother acts like Gram could wake up any minute. She is having an even harder time than I am accepting this."

"That must be very hard on your mom. It's her mother, right?"

"Uh-huh," Carrie said. "They were never very close, and I think my mother feels guilty about that now."

Guilt was an emotion Hope was very familiar with. "Do you have siblings?"

"Two brothers. Todd is in the Marines. He's stationed in Okinawa right now. My brother Sammy lives in North Carolina with his wife and kids. They came to see my grandmother when this first happened, but they couldn't stay long because of their jobs and the kids' school."

"And what about your dad?" Hope asked, hoping she wasn't overstepping with all these questions. She wanted to get to know Carrie better.

"He left when I was ten. The last I heard, he was remarried and living somewhere out West. I don't hear from him much and that's okay with me. He wasn't much of a father when he was around."

"So sorry." Her father was the only one in the family who seemed to be on her side. Hope couldn't imagine her life without him.

Carrie shrugged. "It was a big deal when I was a kid. Took me some time to accept that that's just who he is. I'm better off without him. So, what about you, do you just have the one sister?"

"Yeah. Marcy. She's ten years older than me. Sometimes she acts more like my mother than my sister. She tends to be very opinionated and bossy. I know she means well, but sometimes she drives me crazy." Actually, more than just sometimes.

"That doesn't sound fun. My brothers are both younger than me, so I get to boss them around. Those are the rules. I believe it's on my birth certificate."

"That explains it then."

Carrie smiled. Hope liked the way her eyes lit up when she did.

"Are you from around here originally?" Carrie poured more water in Hope's glass.

"Born and raised. My parents still live in Penfield, in the same house I grew up in. Of course, it was mostly farmland when I was little. We lived next door to a horse farm. It is so built up now. There is a bank or drug store on every corner."

"Do you see your parents often?" Carrie asked.

"Every couple of weeks or so. My dad comes over and helps me with things around the house, yard work, small repairs, and things like that. He was so much help to me when Tom was sick. I'm not sure I could have gotten through it without him." She smiled at the thought of her father.

"I have always wondered what it was like to have a father like that."

"Sorry," Hope said, not really sure what she was sorry for. Maybe it was the hint of hurt in Carrie's voice, despite her earlier statement. "My mother drives me a little crazy." She hoped that would somehow lessen Carrie's pain. "She tends to treat me like I'm still a little kid."

"That can't be easy," Carrie said.

"It's not, but I do my best to ignore her constant *suggestions*, as she calls them." Hope finished the last of the food on her plate.

"Would you like more?" Carrie asked.

"No, thank you. I'm stuffed. That was delicious. You'll have to give me your secret online recipe."

Carrie laughed. "I'll give you the copy I printed. But I have to warn you I got some sauce on it."

"That works."

Hope enjoyed their casual conversation while they cleared the table and loaded the dirty dishes into the dishwasher. Carrie filled a couple of containers with leftovers for Hope to take home with her. "I'm trusting you with my good Tupperware. That means I get to see you again when you return it."

"Or it means you'll lose some good containers."

Hope was sure she would see Carrie again. In fact, she was looking forward to it. She smiled at the thought.

"What are you smiling at?" Carrie asked.

"At the thought of adding to my stolen Tupperware collection."

Carrie playfully swatted at her with a dishtowel.

"Hey. You could hurt me. I'm delicate."

"Delicate like a flower?" Carrie's smile matched her own.

"Nope. Delicate like a bomb."

"Noted. I would hate to see you explode—especially from getting hit with a dishtowel."

"Oh, I think it would take more than a dishtowel."

"Like a two-by-four?"

"Let's not find out. Want to show me those drawings you were telling me about?"

"Absolutely."

"Great. Lead the way." Hope followed Carrie down a small hallway to the room on the end. A slight smell of oil paints and turpentine greeted them as Carrie opened the door.

"Here they are," Carrie said as she led Hope over to the pile of drawings. She spread them out on the table so Hope could get a better look.

"These are great. May I?" she asked before picking one up.

"Sure, go ahead."

"Carrie, I am really impressed. Did you use a model for these or are they out of your head?"

"These are rough sketches out of my head, just to get an idea of how I want the poses to be. If you do decide to model for me, this is basically what I would want you to do. See how I drew in the material here." She pointed to a drawing on the table. "The material covers up the breasts. There isn't any actual nudity. Not that I'm against nudity," Carrie said. "I just want these to be really sensual without being sexual. Does that make sense?"

"Yes." She could put her modesty aside for the sake of art—and spending more time with this new friend. Posing wouldn't be too bad. "I'm seriously considering modeling for you."

Carrie smiled back. "Really? That would be so great. I'm so excited about this."

"You haven't seen me with my clothes off yet. You might change your mind when you do," Hope teased her.

"Stop it. You're going to be perfect for this. It'll be great." Carrie's enthusiasm bubbled to the surface and spread across her face in a big grin.

Hope set the drawing down and glanced around the room. "Can I look at what you are working on?" She pointed at the painting on the easel.

"Feel free to look at whatever you want." Carrie stepped out of the way to give Hope more room to move around. Hope spent a long moment looking at Carrie before walking over to the easel.

Carrie had found herself getting lost in those brown eyes and was grateful when Hope looked away and went over to the painting she was working on. Without her consent, she found herself looking directly at Hope's butt. She forced her eyes away and shook her head. But before she realized it, she found herself once again taking in the sight before her. I'm just checking out the model from an artistic angle, she reasoned. *Stop it. What would she think if she saw you ogling her? And why are you ogling her anyway? You don't ogle. You especially don't ogle straight women.*

"You are an amazing artist," Hope said, turning toward her.

Carrie brought her eyes up quickly. "Thanks."

"How come you don't do this full-time?"

"Because I like to do things like pay my bills and buy groceries. It's really hard to make a living with just the art. I have a day job, but my art is how I keep my sanity."

"Sanity is highly overrated." Hope grinned. "I gave up on it, years ago."

"You're very funny," Carrie said, once more looking into the depth of Hope's eyes. "What do you think of this one?" Carrie found the need to break the eye contact. She led Hope over to another painting—a landscape, not Carrie's favorite thing to paint, but this one was inspired by the way the late afternoon sun bounced off the trees.

"Oh, I like it." She took several long moments to examine it closely before turning back to Carrie.

Carrie felt her face grow warm when she realized she had been studying Hope the whole time Hope had been studying her painting. "Um, should we have dessert? I made red velvet cake. We can have it in the living room." Carrie busied herself stacking the drawings on the table into a pile, trying to get her thoughts in order.

"I love red velvet cake. Keep feeding me like this and you'll have one chubby model."

"I doubt that—and does that mean you've decided?" Carrie worked to keep the excitement out of her voice.

Hope smiled. "I'm leaning toward saying yes."

"I can accept leaning—for now. I really hope you will. Why don't you make yourself comfortable in the living room and I'll go get dessert. Coffee? I have decaf. Or tea?" Carrie shut the lights off and closed the door as they left the room.

"Decaf would be good."

Carrie got everything together and piled it on a serving tray. Hope was examining other paintings that adorned the living room walls when Carrie entered the room. "Here we go." She set the tray on the coffee table and handed Hope her piece of cake.

They sat across from each other, enjoying their dessert and each other's company. The conversation ran the gamut from Carrie's art to Hope's son to Carrie's favorite hand cream.

"I am going to try that one," Hope said. "My hands get so dry. I'm constantly washing them, especially seeing I have my fingers in people's mouths all day long."

"Does that have something to do with what you do for a living or is putting your fingers in people's mouths just a hobby?" Carrie asked with a straight face.

"Yeah, I just do it for fun." Hope grinned. "I'm a dental hygienist, so it kind of comes with the territory. I went back to school when my son started kindergarten. I wanted to do something that wouldn't take forever to get my degree and would bring money into the house. It definitely isn't my passion."

"What is your passion?"

"I guess that would be writing?"

Carrie leaned forward. "Then why don't you write?"

"I went to college with the intention of majoring in journalism. I really wanted to be a writer. I dropped out after my first semester because I was pregnant with Derrick. I got married five months before he was born. I put my career goals on the back burner, so I could take care of him and my husband. *My* ambitions took a back seat to *their* needs. I figured being a dental hygienist would be a good choice because I knew the hours would allow me to be home with them at night." Hope took a bite of her cake and nodded her approval.

"And what about now?"

"Now?" Hope repeated. "Hmm, now I guess I am just where I am. I haven't really thought about it much."

"Do you still write?"

"Poems and an occasional short story. But not in a while. I haven't written in a year or more. I just haven't had anything inspire me lately."

Maybe I could inspire you. Carrie reprimanded herself. What the hell? She chalked it up to her recent feelings of loneliness. Of course, that might have just been an excuse to let herself off the hook for finding herself so attracted to a straight woman and possibly her model. Any kind of feelings for her would just be wrong.

"It's not that I don't have the time. I seem to have plenty of that when I'm not working. It's just—I don't know."

"What do you do with them? Your poems and stories."

"I don't do anything with them. They're just in notebooks, stacked in my closet."

Carrie slipped off her shoes and pulled her feet under her. "I would love to read some if you'd let me. I think it's time they came out of that closet."

"I'm not sure how good they are. I would hate to have them bore you."

"I doubt they would bore me." *'Cause I find you quite interesting.* "But I understand if you don't want to show me. I won't push."

"I'll think about it. How about that?"

"Okay. That's fair." Carrie tilted her head. "Derrick's your only child?"

"One and only. He always wanted a little brother, but I thought one child was enough for me. So, I got him a puppy instead."

Carrie laughed. "And did that satisfy him?"

"No. But it helped. You know how you hear about parents getting their kids a pet and the parents end up doing all the work?"

Carrie nodded. "Oh yeah."

"We got him a puppy—Mork—the cutest little mutt—and Derrick actually took care of it. He was only seven at the time. He just loved that dog to pieces."

"That's great. Do you still have him?"

"No. He actually crossed the rainbow bridge shortly after Tom died." Hope paused, and Carrie sensed her discomfort. "I can't believe I'm telling you this. I cried more over losing that dog than I did over Tom." Hope looked away.

Carrie's heart went out to her. She hesitated only a moment before crossing the space between them and sitting on the couch next to her and laying a hand on hers. "It's okay. You didn't do anything wrong."

Hope cleared her throat. "I feel like a horrible person for my feelings."

"Feelings aren't right or wrong. They just are."

"I appreciate you saying that. I have never shared this with anyone. It was just such a—I don't know—a relief when Tom finally died. He had fought such a long battle. Don't get me wrong, I grieved for my son's loss, but was relieved, not only for me but also for Tom. He was ready to go by that point. He was tired of fighting."

Carrie resisted the urge to hug Hope. She barely knew this woman and as much as she wanted to comfort her she didn't know how Hope would feel about it. "You are being way too hard on yourself. I can tell, even in the short time I've known you, you have a lot of compassion and kindness."

It was Hope who made the first move and pulled Carrie into a hug. "Thank you for not thinking I'm a monster."

Carrie, against her will, felt herself melting into Hope and allowed the hug to go on for only a few seconds. She pulled back, looked into Hope's brown eyes, and said, "You are the exact opposite of a monster." *You are a wonderful woman with a heart of gold and someone I would like to get to know much better.*

CHAPTER SEVEN

Hope tapped her finger on the back of her cell phone, feeling like a stupid teenager. It had been several days since she'd had dinner with Carrie and had revealed *some* of her deepest, darkest feelings. She wanted to call Carrie but didn't really have a reason. She just felt like talking. Hope had many friends throughout the years, but most were friends *with a reason.* They were the mothers of her son's friends, so they talked about the kids. They were the wives of her husband's business partners, so they talked about their husbands. They were friends from her job, so they talked about work.

Carrie was different. She was a friend just because Hope liked her and enjoyed her company. She hadn't had that since college. She hadn't had that since—well, in a really long time.

Hope took a deep breath and hit the call button next to Carrie's name in her contact list. Carrie picked up on the second ring.

"Hi, Hope," Carrie said cheerfully. "How are you doing?"

Hope was pleasantly surprised at Carrie's obvious reaction to her call. At least she hoped the cheeriness was because of her. "I'm good. How are you?"

"Great. I'm so glad you called. I was thinking about you."

Hope couldn't help but smile. "You were, huh? Something good, I hope."

"Very good. I was thinking about how much I enjoyed your company the other night. We'll have to do that again soon."

"I would like that," Hope said. "What are you doing on Friday? We could go out to dinner or I could cook something here. And by cook something here, I mean order from Grubhub."

Carrie laughed. Hope warmed to the sound of it.

"Truth be told, I'm not the best cook," Hope admitted. She seemed to be willing to admit a lot to Carrie. Not quite everything. But a lot.

"In that case, there's a new Sandra Bullock movie I wanted to see. What would you think about going to the movies and then going out and grabbing a bite to eat? Or we could eat first and then see the movie. I don't care which way we do it as long as it involves food." Carrie laughed again. "How does that sound?"

"It sounds good. I haven't gone to the movies in years. In fact, I think the last movie I saw in the theater was—hmmm—*Frozen*.

"Oh yeah, I think you're due. The Sandra Bullock movie is playing at the Plaza Theater. Hang on a sec and I'll tell you the times." Hope could hear the sound of paper rustling. "I'm back. Okay, let's see here. It's playing at seven, nine thirty, and eleven thirty. What do you think?"

"How about we go eat at seven, and we catch the movie at nine thirty?"

"That'll work. Seeing I picked the movie, you pick where we eat."

"All right. I'll check what's around there and let you know. Would you like me to pick you up?" Hope paced back and forth across the living room as she talked. It was a habit she picked up when Derrick was a baby, and the only way to keep him quiet when she was on the phone was to walk with him.

"Sure," Carrie said. "Just let me know where you want to eat, when you know, so I know how to dress. If we are going to Burger King I'll just wear jeans. But if you want to go to La Shareese I might have to pull out my old bridesmaid dress."

Hope laughed enjoying Carrie's humor. "I don't think we're going to Burger King or La Shareese. But I'll be sure to let you know."

"How are you doing? How is Derrick doing? Has he changed girlfriends yet? I'm assuming you've changed your underwear since you met her." This was the reason Hope had wanted to talk to Carrie. She seemed to really care about her and her life—and apparently her underwear. Carrie was certainly a bright spot in her day.

"Yes, I've changed my underwear a time or two since Derrick was here. And yes, as far as I know, she's still his girlfriend. I talked to him this morning and he mentioned her several times. I do believe my son is smitten."

Carrie laughed. "Smitten, huh? Guess that means he likes her."

"What's wrong with the word *smitten*? It's a perfectly good word." Hope feigned being offended.

"Nothing at all, it just sounds like something that would have come out of my grandmother's mouth." Hope could hear the amusement in Carrie's voice.

"I'll take that as a compliment then, because I hear your grandmother is a special lady."

"Yep, that's how I meant it—as a compliment. That's exactly how I meant it."

"I thought so. Speaking of grandmothers, how is she doing? Any change at all?"

"No. I went to see her today. I played her some Lady Gaga music. I figured if anything would bring her out of the coma, that would do it."

"Why, is she a Lady Gaga fan?"

"No, not at all. I thought maybe she would wake up to tell me to turn it off." Hope was silent for a moment, not sure what to say. "You can laugh. I'm just joking. I am trying to keep my humor here."

"Humor is important at a time like this, that's for sure."

They chatted away for close to an hour. Hope found it very easy to talk to Carrie. Her ear was numb by the time she hung up the phone. But she didn't mind.

Hope tossed her cell phone on a chair in the living room and sat at her desk tucked away in the corner. She opened her laptop and googled restaurants. Satisfied with her selection, she closed the computer and pulled an old notebook and pen from the desk drawer. For some reason she found herself in the mood to write. It was a feeling she hadn't had in quite some time. She welcomed it back like a long-lost friend and wondered if her newfound inspiration had anything to do with her newfound friend.

CHAPTER EIGHT

Hope didn't know why she was having such a hard time deciding what to wear. She stood in only her bra and underwear and peered into her closet. The pile of clothes on the bed was growing larger as she tried on another shirt and tossed it on top of the mountain. She pulled a light blue silk blouse from her closet. She held it in front of her and took a look in the full-length mirror. This shirt might work. She slipped her arms into the sleeves and studied herself in the mirror as she did up the buttons. She left the top button undone. She examined herself in the mirror again and undid one more button. It showed more of her throat but didn't come anywhere near showing her cleavage. She undid one more button, added a pendant on a thin silver chain around her neck, and nodded her approval at her reflection.

Guess I should put on a pair of slacks too. Not sure showing up in just my undies would be the best idea. Although I sure would make an entrance. After another quick tour through her closet, she slipped on a pair of dark gray pants with pleats down the front. Satisfied with the way she looked, she set about hanging up the discarded clothes.

Her attention was drawn to the cardboard box on the shelf above her head. She pulled it down and put it on the now cleared off bed. She avoided the layer of dust on top, gently lifted the lid, and set it on the floor. She sat on the bed and pulled out the spiral notebook on top. The bright red cover was smooth under her fingers. She flipped through the pages, stopping here and there to read the words she had written what seemed like a lifetime ago. A poem she had written before Tom's cancer diagnosis caught her eye. If memory served, it was written the day she'd first looked for an apartment for her and Derrick.

Now I don't believe in good fortune
And I don't believe in accidents
And I've gone against all of my instincts
In complete disregard of good sense

And I've put myself in this position
All at good judgment's expense
Since I've accepted this mission
I cannot claim innocence
I should run

Now I stand here before you on guard
Yet we're willing to play this game
These walls that surround me are hard to get through
But I know that you'll try just the same
I should run

You should go your way and I'll go my way
Say it's been nice and move along without delay
I struggle in my head and it argues with my heart every day
I know better that's why I can't stay

I can't help but trust my suspicion
You want more than I'm able to give
But you shouldn't mistake my submission
As love, because it's all relative

Because this broken heart that I carry
Will cause you nothing but grief
I was willing to give you my body
But our moments of joy would be brief
You should run

She shoved the memories to the darkest recesses of her mind. They were not memories she was proud of. There was a lot in her past she wasn't proud of or willing to think about. She set the notebook aside and put the box back on the closet shelf.

Hope slipped her cell phone into her purse, grabbed the notebook, and headed down the stairs. A quick primp in the hallway mirror to fix a stray piece of hair and apply a fresh layer of lipstick and she was on her way.

The traffic on the express was light for a Friday night and the short drive only took her ten minutes. In Carrie's driveway, Hope checked herself one more time in the rearview mirror. Satisfied, she grabbed the notebook from the passenger seat and made her way up the sidewalk to the door. She didn't have to wait long for Carrie, dressed in a tan cardigan and black dress pants, to open it. A simple gold chain around her slender neck completed the look. Her normally straight hair had a bit of a curl to it, and Hope suspected she had used a curling iron.

"Wow, you look nice," Hope said with sincerity.

"You don't look so bad yourself," Carrie replied. "Come on in. I'm just about ready. I have to find my other shoe." She held up a black pump with a low heel.

Hope stepped into the house that now felt familiar. "How could you lose your shoe?"

"I'm usually a T-shirt and sneakers kind of gal. I haven't worn these in quite a while. This one was shoved toward the back of my closet and my closet is a mess, so the other one has to be in there."

"Want help?" Hope pushed the sudden image she had of Carrie on her hands and knees, half in and half out of the closet, from her mind. It startled her.

"Nope. Make yourself at home. Be right back. If I don't find it quick, I'll grab another pair."

Hope barely had time to settle down on the sofa when Carrie returned with a shoe in each hand.

"Found it." She deftly slipped them on without missing a beat and plopped down next to Hope.

Hope handed her the spiral notebook.

"What's this?" Carrie asked, flipping through the pages. "Oh my God. Is this your writing?"

Hope smiled at the delight in her voice. "Don't get too excited. I don't know how good they are. This is mostly poems, but there are a few of my short stories too."

"But I *am* excited. I am so looking forward to reading this." She looked up at Hope. "Can I read one now?"

Hope laughed. Carrie was adorable, acting like a child who had just been handed a present. "I guess you can, but if you don't like it, be gentle. If you tell me it sucks it's going to hurt my feelings."

"It's not going to suck. Stop it." Carrie thumbed through the book, stopping a few pages in. She read the title out loud. "'Feel Again.'"

"I changed my mind. Don't read it now." She felt heat creep up her neck and was sure she was turning bright red. She was suddenly flustered and embarrassed, not exactly sure why.

"Yes. Why not?" Carrie seemed determined. "Close your ears if you don't want to hear it."

Hope just shook her head in defeat. "Okay. Fine."

"'Feel Again,'" Carrie repeated.

"What I would give to once again feel
The hope of my youth and force of my dream
And the faith that once flowed
Through my very blood stream

That bitterness owns now and will not redeem
In the search for my soul all I find is a ghost
Of all that I've lost, I miss myself the most

Some people say they would not change a thing if they could
I'm here to say, that I would, I would, I would
Oh what I would give to have eternal peace and a good
*   night's sleep*
And the silence that comes from so very deep
What I would I give to stop living the past with this heart
*   made of stone*
And to learn to let go of the only love I've ever known

I don't know if this is all said and done or just one of life's
*   interludes*
I've persevered longer than most anyone
So pray for this hopeless cause to St. Jude

"Wow, Hope. That is so good. That is so good," Carrie said.

"Thank you." The heat once again rose to her face.

"I mean it. I can't wait to read the rest."

Hope stood. "Well, don't read them now. I'm hungry. Are you ready to go?"

"Okay. Okay." She set the notebook on the coffee table. Hope offered her a hand, which Carrie accepted and let herself be pulled up off the couch.

Hope tried to ignore the warmth of Carrie's hand in hers. She let go, maybe a little too abruptly, and headed toward the door.

❖

Hope liked the restaurant as soon as they stepped in from the chilly night air. The warm and inviting feel to it was only enhanced by the smell of fresh tomato sauce and grilled steak.

They were seated almost immediately once Hope told the maître d' they had reservations. She was grateful for her foresight. They bypassed several people waiting for tables. A large double-sided fireplace, centrally situated, added a soft glow to the dark, rich wood that lined the walls, giving the place an elegant yet rustic look.

The waiter arrived within moments delivering menus, a basket of fresh bread, and a pitcher of ice water, which he left on their table once he had filled their glasses. He rattled off the specials with the slightest hint of a Boston accent, giving the impression he had worked hard to lose it.

"This is my treat, so order anything you want," Hope said.

Carrie put down her menu. "In that case, I'll have the lobster, steak, the most expensive bottle of wine, and two servings of tiramisu for dessert."

"All right then. As long as you're sure." Carrie's smile lit up her face. Hope was struck by her beauty. "I guess I'll just have water then, because I'm not going to be able to afford two meals if you're going to order all that."

"Oh sure, offer me food and then make me feel guilty about it. I guess I'll just get the grilled salmon and a cheap glass of wine."

"How about you get the grilled salmon and a decent glass of wine?" Hope picked up her menu.

"And maybe we can share a tiramisu for dessert?" Carrie raised her eyebrows.

"If you behave."

The waiter returned to the table in short time. "Are you ready to order?" He was tall, with dark eyes and a handsome smile. His tanned skin appeared even darker against his white dress shirt.

"We are." Hope nodded. "Go ahead, Carrie."

Carrie ordered her meal and a glass of chardonnay.

"I'll have the same but no wine. Can I get lemon for my water?"

"Of course."

Hope reached for Carrie's menu and handed both to him. "Thanks." Hope turned her attention back to her dinner companion. "How was your day?"

"Good. I snuck out of work early and did a little painting." She leaned forward and whispered, "But don't tell anyone."

Hope whispered back, "I won't."

Now it was Carrie's turn to ask. "And how was your day? Did you remember to wash your hands after every mouth?"

"Yes, I washed after every mouth." Hope grinned. "My day was good. We had two last-minute cancellations, so I got to leave on time, which doesn't always happen."

"You did a great job picking the restaurant by the way. I've heard they have great food."

"I'm glad. I've never been here before."

Carrie looked surprised. "How come you picked a place you've never been to?"

"I looked up places online. I wanted some place nice, but not so nice that you had to wear your bridesmaid's dress. The thought of that just scared me." Hope gave a laugh that was matched by Carrie's. "I looked at what got good reviews. This place came out on top."

The fire nearby cast a warm glow on Carrie's skin and danced in her green eyes. Hope felt lost in those eyes for a long moment. *Carrie is a beautiful woman. Anyone would notice how smooth her skin looks and how green her eyes are.* Hope justified the thoughts to herself, and she believed it—at least for a little while.

The restaurant turned out to be a good choice. The food was delicious and there wasn't enough left to take home doggy bags. After taking the dirty dishes away, the waiter returned with one tiramisu and two spoons. Carrie dipped her spoon into the dessert and took a bite. "Mmm, this is so good," she said, her hand covering her full mouth. She took another spoonful and offered it across the table to Hope.

Hope leaned in and accepted the offering. She nodded her approval. They finished the desert in record time, and Hope was very full and extremely satisfied when they made their way back to Hope's car. She assumed Carrie felt the same.

The short car ride to the theater was comfortably quiet. Carrie bought their tickets, holding up her hand to silence any protests from Hope. They passed by the large movie posters, boosting upcoming films and made their way to theater five. The previews hadn't yet started, and Hope was glad lights were still on, making it easier for them to choose their seats. And there were still plenty of seats to choose from. "Where would you like to sit?" Carrie asked.

"Somewhere toward the middle. Not too close to the screen."

"Perfect."

They'd only taken a few steps in when the room was plunged into darkness. The movie screen lit up with a warning about talking and turning off your cell phone during the movie. A dim light bounced off the screen. Hope's eyes didn't adjust to the change in darkness as fast as Carrie's seemed to and she reached out and grabbed Carrie's hand as she realized Carrie was moving forward without her. If Carrie minded, she didn't say anything.

"How's this? Not too close."

"It's fine," Hope said into Carrie's ear as music from the first preview filled the room, aware Carrie's hand was still in hers. Warm. Comforting. She let go of Carrie's hand and ran her own hand through her hair. She refused to let her mind think about how good Carrie's hand felt in hers. She sat and turned her attention to the screen.

Hope thoroughly enjoyed her evening with Carrie. The food and conversation at the restaurant were wonderful, and she had enjoyed the movie. Romantic comedies were her favorites and Sandra Bullock never disappointed. She was sorry to see the night end as she pulled into Carrie's driveway. "Well, here we are," she said.

"Would you like to come in for something to drink?" Carrie asked, "Or a snack?"

"I would love to, but I really should get going." It wasn't that she didn't want to go in. She did. She wasn't exactly sure why she'd said no.

"Okay." Carrie leaned across the small chasm between them and gave Hope a hug. "I had a great time. Thanks so much. Drive careful." Her smile was bright, even in the darkness of the car.

"I had a great time, too. Have a good night."

Hope waited and watched Carrie walk down the sidewalk and unlock her door. She returned the wave Carrie sent her way and watched her go in. She sat in her car for several long moments simultaneously trying to gather her thoughts and push unwelcomed thoughts away, before backing out onto the street and heading home to what seemed tonight to be an extremely empty house.

❖

Carrie slipped her shoes off at the door. She poured herself the last glass of wine from the bottle Hope had brought for dinner the week before and made herself comfortable on the couch. With her feet tucked under her, she reached for the notebook with Hope's poems and short stories and began to read.

It was two a.m. by the time Carrie looked up from the notebook and was shocked at how quickly the time had flown. She was only halfway through it. The rest would have to wait till another time. She set it on the coffee table, rose, and stretched to remove the kinks.

If she liked Hope before—and she did—she liked her even more now. Reading her words, Carrie felt like she'd seen a glimpse into Hope's soul, a soul full of love and kindness and at the same time full of want and a life unfulfilled.

She made her way to the bedroom, stripped out of her clothes, and slipped on an old T-shirt and sweatpants that she used as pajamas. She was asleep almost as soon as her head hit the pillow. But her sleep was fitful as her dreams were filled with images of Hope. Those images faded into tiny sliver-like memories when she woke with the morning light. She struggled to put the slivers back into a full picture. But like an old used puzzle, there were many pieces missing.

CHAPTER NINE

I read your notebook. I really, really like your writing," Carrie said. It was turning out to be a beautiful day for a walk on the canal. Hope was glad she had remembered to bring her sunglasses. The trail wasn't very crowded for a Saturday. Of course, there were always fewer people out in the fall than in the summer. It had been a little more than a week since their dinner and a movie. Since then, they had spent several evenings talking on the phone, their conversations often moving from serious, personal topics to light, humorous ones that sent them both into fits of laughter.

"Thank you," Hope said. She hadn't realized how nervous she'd been at the prospect of Carrie reading her work until she recognized how relieved she felt at that moment. She felt like she could breathe again. "I've never let anyone read my writing before."

"No one?" Carrie's voice betrayed her surprise.

"No. I guess my writing has been like a private piece of me I kept for myself," Hope said.

Carrie stopped walking. Hope took another two steps before realizing she was walking alone and stopped. She turned back toward Carrie. Carrie just looked at her.

"What?" Hope asked.

"You never showed them to anyone, ever? But you let *me* read them? Wow. I am truly honored." She took a step closer to Hope and touched her arm. "Why me?"

Hope shrugged. She couldn't quite put into words how close she felt to Carrie and why she had let her read what no one else even knew existed. "I guess because I trust you." She looked up at the deep blue sky and tried to find the right words to explain. "I knew they would be safe in your hands." She searched Carrie's face to see if her words were making sense. When she found they were, she went on. "I feel like my heart is on those pages. I…" Hope stammered. "I kept my heart in that box, in the closet along with my notebooks. Maybe I thought it was time to let it out. I trusted you wouldn't read my words and think I was a fool."

"Thank you for that. I would never think you're a fool. You are a wonderful person and an excellent writer, and I think you should try to get your work published." They began to walk again.

"I'm not sure about that," Hope said.

"Why? Because it's so personal?"

"No, because I'm not sure it's good enough." It was one thing letting Carrie read it. It was another letting the whole world into her heart and possibly having it torn to shreds.

Carrie reached for Hope's arm again. "Believe me, it's more than good enough."

Hope looked down where Carrie's hand touched bare skin. The warmth and comfort it brought mingled with the edge of fear. It brought back a memory Hope had long ago pushed aside. She felt both a longing and relief when Carrie let go of her arm.

They walked in relative silence for several minutes, with only the sounds of the birds and the frogs filling in the gap.

"Would you like to read more of my writing?" Hope asked as they got to a paved section of the trail. The area ahead was the backdrop for several restaurants and specialty shops.

"Absolutely. I would love to."

Hope wasn't surprised. Carrie was turning out to be the support she never seemed to have before. When she said she trusted her, she meant it. She knew her writing and her deepest thoughts—well, most of them—would be safe.

"Want to buy me a cup of coffee?" Hope asked in an attempt to change the subject. Trusting Carrie was one thing. Trusting in the quality of her own writing was another.

"Sure. How about this place? Which by coincidence just happens to be a coffee shop. They walked around to the front of the small building. Carrie held open the door and made a sweeping motion with her arm for Hope to enter.

The smell of warm coffee and a hint of vanilla enveloped them, giving Hope a feeling of comfort. A large blackboard behind the counter listed off their beverage choices. Some creative employee had drawn out various pictures of coffee beans, muffins, and steaming cups in colorful chalk.

"What'll you have?" The tall teenager behind the counter was in bad need of a haircut.

"Medium vanilla low-fat latte," Hope said. She turned to Carrie. "Want to split a piece of coffee cake?"

"No. I want my own piece." Carrie winked.

Hope couldn't help but laugh.

Carrie turned to the teenager. "Two pieces of coffee cake and I'll have a cup of, umm, let's see..." She looked the board over again. "A cinnamon caramel latte. Medium." She paid him and tucked a couple of dollar bills and the loose change he gave her back into the tip jar.

Carrie grabbed both plates the boy set on the counter. "Want to sit while we wait for the coffee?" She nodded toward one of the last two tables left unoccupied. Hope led the way and pulled out a chair for Carrie. The nearby window allowed them to enjoy the sun without being directly in its bright rays. The soft sounds of classical music floated through the air giving an overall sense of peacefulness.

It didn't take long before their coffees were ready, and Hope went to get them.

"It turned out to be a really nice day, didn't it?" Carrie said. "Nice day, good coffee." She held up her cup. "Great company."

Hope agreed. She couldn't have asked for a better day or better friend to spend it with.

They sat and talked for quite a while. Most of the customers who were there when they arrived had been replaced by other people by the time they returned their empty plates to the counter and threw their paper coffee cups away.

Carrie led the way to a small novelty shop next door. "I love this place," she said as they entered. The small store was crammed full of handmade items that ran the gamut from delicate crocheted baby blankets to hand painted rocks.

"Oh, this is beautiful," Carrie said, picking up a glass Christmas tree ornament. Hope nodded in agreement before wandering over to a selection of hand carved figurines.

Carrie strolled through the shop, stopping here and there to examine some of the merchandise a little closer. By the cash register, she spotted several very elegant looking pens. Each one was individually packaged in a box made of the same wood that the pen was made from. She gingerly picked one up. The smoothness and weight felt good in her hand. The small label hanging from a string tied to the pen announced the pen was made from zebrawood. Other pens were made from oak, walnut, or ash. Carrie definitely liked the look of the zebrawood the best.

"Aren't they superb?" the plump woman behind the counter asked her.

"They are," Carrie agreed.

The woman pulled a pad of paper from under the counter and set it in front of her. "Here," she said. "Go ahead and write with it. Give it a try."

Carrie wrote her name and drew a few squiggles on the paper. The ink flow was smooth and even. "I'll take it," Carrie said, lowering her voice. "Do you have gift wrapping? It's going to be a gift for my friend over there." She subtly tilted her head toward Hope.

"Of course," the woman whispered back.

Carrie gently put the pen back into the box and closed the lid. She handed it to the woman, followed by her credit card.

"I'll be right back," the woman told Carrie after she ran her credit card. She slipped through a doorway behind the counter, taking the pen with her.

Carrie's attention was drawn to a display of hand painted rocks on a table to the left of the counter. She picked up a rock with a tricolored collie painted on it. The irregular shape of the rock lent itself perfectly to the outline of the dog. She examined the painting closely.

"Those are painted by a local artist, Christine Darna. I just love them." The saleswoman had returned. She discreetly handed Carrie a small bag containing a neatly wrapped package.

"She puts so much detail into them. I swear I'm going to feel fur when I touch them," the woman continued.

"It's really beautifully painted," Carrie said, turning the rock over in her hand.

"And see how she matches the subject to the shape of the rock?" The saleswoman grabbed another rock sporting a painting of a squirrel. It was almost as if the rock had been created just for that painting. "Do you have a collie?"

"No, my grandmother did. She loved—loves them. How much is this?"

"Twenty-four ninety-five, plus tax of course. Always got to give the government their share. I'm sure your grandmother would love it."

Carrie glanced over at Hope. She was busy looking through a rack of hand drawn greeting cards. She mulled over the idea of adding another collie to the collection her mother had started for her grandmother. "Oh, what the heck," she said, "I'll take it."

The woman carefully wrapped it in tissue paper as if it were fine crystal and gently placed it into a small red bag with paper handles. Carrie deposited the bag with the gift-wrapped pen into it.

"What are you buying?" Hope asked as she approached the counter.

"Another collie for my grandmother's collection. I think I am starting to be as crazy as my mother. But it was so cute, I couldn't help myself."

"Nothing wrong with crazy."

"Oh yeah. Do you know that personally?"

"You haven't realized by now how crazy I am?"

Carrie laughed. Crazy or not, she was starting to really like Hope.

CHAPTER TEN

I need you to take all your clothes off."

"You aren't even going to buy me dinner first?" Hope said. "Usually my dates buy me dinner before ordering me to get naked."

"Hey, I bought you coffee last week and I gave you a snack when you got here. What more do you want?" Carrie adjusted the blinds on the window, letting more light into the room. Her tone turned more serious as she gave her full attention to Hope. "Not too late to back out if you don't feel comfortable with it."

Hope gave her a reassuring grin. "I'm kidding. I'm fine."

"Okay. I'll leave the room and you can get undressed. You can leave your underpants on for this part, but your bra needs to come off." Carrie handed Hope a neatly folded length of light blue satin about six inches wide and ten feet long. "You can wrap this around you, so you're covered and call me when you're ready. I have the heat turned up, so you shouldn't get chilled." She looked into Hope's brown eyes and noticed the tiny gold flakes reflected in them. Beautiful eyes, she thought to herself, beautiful woman. Straight woman, she reminded herself. "Ready to do this?" Carrie asked her.

"Ready as I'll ever be."

Carrie left the room and closed the door behind her. She leaned back and rested her head against it. She let out a breath, doing her best to get her wits about her. She had to focus on the fact that Hope was her model. Not someone she was interested in. It didn't matter how beautiful she was. Her model. Her friend. Nothing more. Not now. Not ever.

Hope took a deep breath. She wasn't overly modest and being naked didn't bother her, but for some reason she wanted Carrie to find her body pleasing. *I'm sure I just want to look nice for the painting.* That seemed plausible enough. Yes. That's what it was.

She removed her blouse, folded it, and placed it on a chair in the corner. The rest of her clothes, except for her underpants, followed. She wrapped the satin cloth loosely around her, covering her breasts and letting it fall over her waist. It didn't quite cover all of her hips. She held it in place with her hands.

Hope called out. "All right. I'm ready." It only took a moment for Carrie to return.

"Perfect," Carrie said.

The heat rose from Hope's chest to her face as Carrie looked her up and down.

"Just need some light," Carrie said, more to herself than to Hope. She pulled a light stand closer and pointed it in the direction of a tall wooden stool positioned a few feet in front of the window. "Okay," she said. "Come on over here and sit." She patted the stool. "I'll pose you."

Hope did as she was told. "Pose away."

"Can you put one foot on the bottom rung of the stool and let the other hang free, touching the floor?" Hope positioned herself on the stool. "Great. Now turn your face this way a little." Carrie gently lifted Hope's chin. She placed a hand on each side of Hope's head to tilt it a little to the left. She felt the warmth of Carrie's hands on her skin, and it sent a chill through her. Hope closed her eyes and swallowed, willing the feeling away. "You okay?" Carrie asked.

Hope opened her eyes. "Yep, just fine." She stared past Carrie and found a spot on the far wall to focus her attention on.

"I am going to need to rearrange the cloth now." Carrie waited until Hope nodded before she continued. She pulled the cloth away from Hope's body, briefly exposing her nakedness. Hope brought her attention back to Carrie and noticed Carrie's eyes remained on the cloth as she moved it over Hope's shoulders and laid it back down covering Hope's breasts. Carrie let out a small sigh. She took the remaining material and arranged it so it covered half of Hope's waist and the tail end of it was laid across Hope's lap. "I am going to pull your underwear down a little on the side here. Okay?"

"Sure. That's fine." Hope continued to watch as Carrie tugged her underwear down a couple of inches exposing the skin on Hope's hip. She arranged the rest of the material, so it covered the underwear and draped down over part of Hope's legs.

Carrie stepped back to take a better look, Hope assumed. She slowly nodded her approval and smiled. "I think that's it. Are you comfortable?"

"Yep," Hope said, staying as still as possible.

"Okay. I'm going to take some photos, so I have something to work from when you aren't here, and then I'm going to start a pencil sketch. It will probably be about thirty minutes before we get a break, but let me know if you need to move before that."

"All right," Hope said, barely moving her mouth.

Carrie laughed. "It's okay to talk, at least right now. So just relax."

"All right," Hope said. "Should I smile or not smile?" She smiled wide and then dropped the corners of her mouth. She smiled again, waiting for Carrie's reply.

"Anything you want is fine at this point. When I get into the details of the face I will let you know what to do." Carrie grabbed her camera from a nearby table and fired off a few shots. After a quick review of the pictures, she adjusted the cloth on Hope's shoulder and snapped a few more. "How ya doing?"

"So far so good." *How do you think I'm doing? And while we're at it, what do you think of my body? Is it good enough?* Hope shook the thoughts from her head. *Stop it. You're being ridiculous.*

"You are doing great." Carrie said, as if reading her mind.

Carrie moved to her easel. "I just need to get a few more from over here so I have the correct view." She pushed the shutter several more times. Carrie did a quick review of the photos and set the camera aside.

Pencil in hand, she looked at Hope for several long moments before making a few broad sweeping strokes on the drawing pad, set upright on the easel in front of her. "Doing okay still?"

"I'm fine. Stop worrying about me. You just draw and make me look beautiful." Hope smiled.

"That won't be hard to do because you really are beautiful, especially when you smile like that," Carrie said.

The compliment went right to Hope's heart. It threatened to move downward, but Hope stopped it in its tracks. "Thanks." She averted her eyes afraid Carrie might read something in them.

"Don't be embarrassed. I have seen hundreds, maybe thousands of beautiful naked women, and you rate right up there in the top one or two percent."

"Thousands, huh?" Hope brought her eyes back to Carrie's. "And where did you happen to see all of these women?" Hope felt a confusing pang of jealousy, despite the fact she knew Carrie was joking.

Carrie's pencil continued to sweep across the paper. "Okay, I might be exaggerating. It was probably more like nine or ten.

Models for my drawing classes in college. And now that I think about it, you are definitely the most beautiful one." She paused for a moment. "Really."

Hope swallowed down the lump that was forming in her throat.

Several minutes passed in silence while Carrie sketched, her eyes traveling between Hope and her sketchpad.

"So, how is everything going? How is work?" Carrie said, startling Hope out of her thoughts.

"Work's fine for the most part, but I did something really stupid."

"I can't imagine that. What did you do?" Carrie's pencil was still as she focused her attention on Hope.

"They're starting a bowling team for our office, and when they asked me to join, I said I would." She shook her head. "Actually, I told them no at first, but they kept bugging me because they were one person short. They wore me down and I gave in."

"And why exactly is that a stupid thing to do?" Carrie resumed her sketching.

"Because I don't bowl. Not really. I haven't since I was a teenager. And even then, I sucked."

"You're in luck then, because I am a great bowler. Not just a good bowler, I mean a great bowler. Do you know what a turkey is?"

"It's three strikes in a row, isn't it?" Hope's nose was beginning to itch.

"Oh yeah, that, too. I was thinking of the big heavy bird we eat at Thanksgiving. I was just testing your knowledge of animals." Carrie giggled at her lame joke.

"You're a turkey," Hope said, laughing.

"Back to my bowling tales. I really am a decent bowler, and if you beg me I can teach you. So what do you say? Want to beg me?"

Hope thought about it for only a moment. "Oh please, oh please, oh please teach me to bowl. How was that? Was that good begging?"

"Wow, that was great. Okay, I'll do it, seeing you asked so nice. When does the league start?"

"Next week." Hope shook her head. "Crazy right?"

"Next week? We better get moving on this then. What are you doing tomorrow?" Carrie examined her sketch, moved her stool back, and examined it again.

Hope tried to look over the top of the sketchpad to see if she could see anything. She couldn't.

"Having breakfast with my mother and sister at nine, but I'm free the rest of the day. What were you thinking?"

"I'm thinking you didn't invite me out to breakfast with your mother and sister."

Hope laughed. "Believe me, I did you a favor not inviting you. A good time will not be had by all. I can take my sister and my mother each by themselves, but together they make me crazy. They don't stop talking and they always have better ideas on how I should run my life than I do."

"Then tomorrow when you can't take any more you just tell them you have to leave because you have a date with a really good looking, really hot bowling coach and you come and get me. And then we bowl, baby. We bowl." Carrie stood and threw an imaginary bowling ball down an imaginary lane.

"Wow. You are good. Great form."

"Told ya." Carrie pulled her stool back to her easel and sat.

"I plan on leaving there around eleven. How about I come and get you at eleven thirty? If you're serious about helping me."

"Of course I'm serious. When have you ever known me not to be serious?" Carrie crossed her eyes and stuck out her tongue. "But seriously," she said, "I would love to help. And eleven thirty would be fine. Now hold your head still for a couple of minutes and then I'll let you take a break."

Hope did as she was told but watched Carrie out of the corner of her eye. She could see Carrie squinting.

"How come you squint?" she asked trying not to move her lips.

"'Cause, that reduces you to blurry shapes and values. It eliminates fine detail."

"Just what I wanted—to have my fine detail eliminated."

"Tip your head up a little and slightly to the left—a little more," Carrie said. "Look up a bit."

Hope followed her instructions.

"Right there. Perfect." Carrie drew for a few more minutes. "Okay, that's it for now. Hang on and I'll get you a robe to put on." Carrie disappeared and returned with a soft pink robe and handed it to Hope.

"Thanks.

Carrie turned her back while Hope slipped off the stool, unwrapped the cloth, and pulled the robe on. "All set," she said, tying the belt around her waist.

Carrie turned back. "Would you like some tea? I have regular, herbal, and a few flavored. And of course, I have fresh baked cookies."

Hope followed Carrie to the kitchen. "Herbal tea—any kind—would be great and I guess I could force one of your cookies down."

Carrie surveyed the cupboard. "How about berry hibiscus?"

"Sounds good."

Hope retied the belt on the bathrobe, pulling it tighter before sitting at the table. The last thing she wanted was for one of her girls to come spilling out.

She watched as Carrie put the teakettle on to boil and took two cups from the shelf. She couldn't help but notice the smooth skin that peeked out between Carrie's pants and her shirt as she reached up.

"Help yourself to the cookies," Carrie said.

Hope pulled her attention away from Carrie and grabbed the nearest cookie from the plate on the table.

They sat and talked until the whistle on the kettle pierced the air. "That is such an obnoxious noise," Carrie said, removing it from the burner. "Would you like milk, or sugar? Or I think I have some honey." She set a cup of tea in front of Hope.

"Nope, it's fine just like this."

"Tell me the truth. Are you comfortable posing? Warm enough?" Carrie joined Hope at the table.

"It's fine. The time goes fast because we talk. When I modeled for art classes back in college, the room was always totally quiet. No music or anything. The only thing you could hear was the professor's shoes squeaking as he walked around the room. It drove me crazy and I felt like time stood still. This is so much better. I don't mind this at all."

"Good," Carrie said, "I would hate it if you were uncomfortable. You make a great model. I think these paintings are going to come out nice."

Hope was delighted.

It didn't take long for them to finish their tea and cookies and head back to the art room. Carrie helped Hope into the correct position and started again on her preliminary drawing.

They talked continuously as Carrie drew, her attention going between the drawing in front of her and Hope. After a while, Carrie said, "It should be just about break time, but if you can stay like that for about ten more minutes, we can call it a night. I think I'll have enough to start the underpainting from this."

"That's fine," Hope replied. She had been so lost in conversation she totally forgot she hadn't moved in quite a while.

It took Carrie another fifteen minutes to finish the drawing. "Sorry about that, took a little longer than I thought," Carrie said as she stood. "Go ahead and get dressed. I'll meet you back in the living room."

Hope was a little stiff as she slipped off the stool. She twisted her neck and shoulders to loosen them, folded the blue cloth, and left it on the stool. As nervous as she had been, this turned out to be not too bad. Fun in fact. Carrie made it enjoyable. Hope found herself looking forward to their next modeling session.

CHAPTER ELEVEN

Carrie couldn't help but laugh at the disgusted look on Hope's face as Hope sat on the hard bench and slipped the bowling shoes on her feet.

"What are you doing?" she asked Hope.

"Are you sure these are sanitary?" Hope asked. "I'm feeling kind of gross putting them on?"

"They spray them after every customer. At least that's the theory. If you want, we can buy you your own pair before we practice next time."

Hope stood. "Yes. I want to do that. Can we get them right now?"

"No." Carrie laughed again. "We can't go now. You'll just have to take your chances that you won't catch some fatal disease from those, because right now we're going to practice."

"But they're so ugly. Ugly, germ-infested bowling shoes." Hope whined but followed Carrie to the lane they'd been assigned.

"Since when are you a germaphobe? You play in people's mouth's all day. I would think you would be very used to germs."

"I'm not a germaphobe. It's just the thought of putting my feet into shoes that have been worn by millions of other people is gross."

"I doubt millions of people have worn that pair of shoes. It probably wasn't more than ten thousand." Carrie was enjoying teasing Hope.

"You aren't helping here."

"Come on, we have to get to work. Forget about the shoes for now." She unzipped the bowling ball bag she brought, pulled out the sixteen-pound ball, and handed it to Hope. "How does that feel?" she asked her.

Hope seemed to think about it for a moment. "It feels hard and round."

"Ha, ha," Carrie said. "I mean the weight. Is it too heavy?"

"Yeah, I am thinking it is." She put her fingers and thumb into the holes and held it up with obvious difficulty. "Yeah, it's too heavy. I feel like such a wimp."

"You're no wimp," Carrie reassured her. "We'll find you a ball that works. Come on." They checked out the rack of balls by the wall. Carrie picked up several balls and examined them, feeling the weight of each in her hands. She handed Hope a twelve-pound ball with pink and white swirls. "What do you think of this one?"

"It's pretty," Hope said with a smile. "But that's probably not what you meant, huh?"

"Smart-ass. No, I meant the weight and finger holes."

Hope slipped her fingers and thumb into it. They slid in easily. She held the ball for several seconds. "This one's fine."

"Let's give it a try then."

Carrie settled down on one of the seats. "Okay, lady, show me what you got."

"You aren't going to show me how to do it first?" Hope's frown reminded Carrie of a disappointed child. It was endearing.

"No, I want to see what you can do first. So, go ahead and I'll watch."

Hope held the ball, right hand gripping it, left hand supporting it from underneath. So far, so good. She took three awkward steps forward, stopped completely and swung her right arm down and back. She flipped her hand completely over, so her thumb faced down when she released the ball. Not so good.

The ball traveled a short distance, then landed with a slight thud in the gutter to continue its journey down the alley. Hope watched the ball until it was completely out of sight, the pins were lifted in the air, and the pin sweeper did its job before turning to Carrie. "How many points was that?"

Carrie tried her best not to laugh but a small snort escaped anyway. "Um, let me think. Gutter balls are zero points, I think." She couldn't hold back the laugh this time. Hope joined her.

"I told you I suck at this."

"That's why I'm here, to help you suck less."

Hope's bowling ball made its rounds and was safely deposited back on the ball return. Carrie retrieved it before Hope had a chance.

"Let's start with holding the ball the right way." She handed the ball to Hope.

Hope slipped her fingers and thumb into the holes and held the ball up to her nose.

Carrie placed her hand on top of Hope's and did her best to ignore the soft skin she was touching. *She's straight, and technically, you hired her to pose for you. Making her your employee. Get any other thoughts out of your head.* She turned her mind back to the task at hand. "Lower the ball and move this hand over here to the side."

Hope did as she was told.

"Okay, that's the way you should hold the ball." Carrie moved so she was behind Hope. "Remember this game is about accuracy. It's not a race. We're going to go nice and slow. You want to be in control." Carrie gently grabbed Hope's waist. "Let's move back a little." She stepped back and moved Hope with her. "Good, now start from here."

Carrie stepped away. "Now take four steps to the line, start on your right foot. As you step you are letting the ball swing back, nice and easy. Straight back and straight forward. Bend your knees a little on the fourth step and let the ball go. Don't worry about where it goes right now. Let's just worry about getting the rhythm of the steps and letting the ball swing."

Hope did everything Carrie had told her. She counted her steps to the foul line out loud, letting the ball swing back and forth with the steps. She let it go and it bounced once before skittering down the alley and into the gutter.

"Much better," Carrie told her. "But you let the ball go a little too late. Here, let me show you. Come on back here to start."

Carrie put her left arm around Hope's waist from behind. With her right hand, she took Hope's hand in her own. "We are going to walk through this." They were so close that Carrie could smell the faded scent of honeysuckle shampoo.

In unison, they took four slow steps. Carrie guided Hope's hand back and then forward again. "When your hand is here…" Carrie said, stopping her hand for a moment, "…is when you let it go. Keep your hand in this position. Don't let it turn." She stayed close behind Hope for a moment longer before letting her go and stepping away.

Carrie retrieved the bowling ball and handed it to Hope. "Give it another try."

Hope took the ball but made no move to throw it. "Can you show me a few times so I can watch you?"

"Amateurs." Carrie shook her head. She retrieved her own ball and walked to her starting point. "I'm starting a little closer than you because my legs are shorter, so my steps are shorter." She narrated her movements as she went. "See where I'm holding the ball. I'm looking down the alley at a spot just left of the head pin. That's what works for me. We'll figure out later what works best for you." The ball slid smoothly down the lane, taking a slight curve to the left before hitting squarely on the head pin, sending most of the pins flying. The seven pin in the corner teetered back and forth before settling back down in an upright position.

Hope clapped her hands. "Excellent."

"Thanks." She rolled her second ball, easily taking out the seven pin, explaining where she was aiming and why. "That's a spare. Are you ready to try again?"

"Yep."

"Okay, let's work on your stance. Release and accuracy come later." She took a couple of steps back. "Do you want me to talk you through it again?"

"Would you mind? Just until I get the hang of this."

Carrie narrated each move and Hope followed her directions. She made steady progress throughout the lesson.

"Now that we have the basics down, the only thing left to do is practice, practice, practice." Carrie paused. "Did I mention you need to practice?"

"A time or two. Yes. And coincidently, that's the same way you get to Carnegie Hall," Hope said.

"Funny lady. What are you doing tomorrow night?"

"Practicing?"

"Hey, that's a good idea. I'm free if you would like help."

"I would really appreciate it." Hope smiled. "but can we go get a pair of my own bowling shoes first?"

"Oh sure. We can go as soon as you get out of those disgusting, germ infested ones," Carrie pointed at the rented shoes on Hope's feet.

"See? I told you."

"You should probably burn those socks when you get home. You know how cooties like to travel."

"Stop."

Carrie laughed. "I'm just funning ya." She wrapped her arm around Hope's shoulder. "Let's go get you shoes and see what other trouble we can get ourselves in to."

CHAPTER TWELVE

Carrie heard the car pull into the driveway and opened the door before Hope even had a chance to knock. "Are you excited?" she asked by way of a greeting.

"More like terrified."

"Stop. You're going to do great. You've come a long way."

"Are you ready to go?"

"Just about. Come on in. I need two more minutes," Carrie said. "I just got home from visiting my grandmother and I need to change." She led the way to the living room.

"Don't. I like you just the way you are."

"My clothes. I need to change my clothes." She smiled. "Sit, make yourself comfortable, and I will be right back."

"You must be hungry," Hope called to her from the living room.

"A little bit," Carrie yelled back. She emerged a few minutes later wearing her favorite jeans and a dark blue long-sleeved T-shirt.

Hope was sitting on the couch with her coat buttoned up to the neck.

"You didn't even take your coat off. Aren't you getting too warm sitting there?"

"Umm, I'm a little embarrassed about my shirt," Hope said.

Carrie smiled. "What do you mean? Is it really low cut or something?" *That I would like to see.*

"No, it's really ugly?"

"Why are you wearing an ugly shirt?"

"It's our team bowling shirt. I can't believe they are making us wear these."

"Well, seeing you are bowling in your league tonight for the first time, I think wearing the team shirt is only right. Let me see it." Hope made a face and Carrie tried not to laugh. She wasn't very successful.

"I'm not sure I want anyone to see it," Hope said.

"I'm not just anyone. Are you planning on bowling with your coat on all night?"

"Maybe," Hope said, standing. "Ready to go?"

"We can go right after you show me the shirt. Come on. Let's see it. It can't be that bad."

"The only thing that will be more embarrassing than my bowling tonight is going to be this shirt."

Carrie stepped toward Hope and unbuttoned the top two buttons on her coat. She stopped as suddenly as she started. The move felt much too intimate and personal. She overstepped. Heat rushed to her face. She wasn't sure if it was embarrassment or from being this close to Hope. "Sorry," she stammered, unsure of what else to say.

"It's all right," Hope reassured her. She unbuttoned the rest of her coat and pulled it open, revealing a shocking orange bowling shirt with her name embroidered above the pocket on the left.

"Wow," Carrie said, doing her best not to laugh. "It sure is bright." She took a step backward to get a better look. "It brings out the brown in your eyes."

"Yeah, thanks," Hope smiled. "I think I'll wear this color more often. I am always looking for clothes that bring out the color of my eyes. The back is even worse. But you're going to have to wait until we get there to see it, because we have to go so we aren't late."

"I'm ready," Carrie said. She grabbed her coat from the closet, and they headed out the door.

"I'll buy you a hotdog and beer for dinner, while you watch me make a fool of myself bowling." She hit the button on her key fob to unlock the doors.

"Deal. But you aren't going to make a fool of yourself. You are going to do fine." Carrie slid into the passenger seat.

"Keep telling me that. A few more times and I might start to believe it. I'm really nervous about this," she admitted. "I am so glad you're going with me."

"Any time." Carrie touched Hope's shoulder. "You *are* going to be just fine," Carrie repeated. "Honest."

"Thank you," Hope said. "For everything."

Everyone from Hope's team was already there when they got to the bowling alley. Carrie thought Hope actually looked very cute in her bowling shirt, at least compared to the rest of her team. All five had on the same ugly orange shirts with the words *JENSON DENTISTRY* with a large white tooth embroidered on the back.

Hope sat and put on her new bowling shoes, wiggled her toes, and appreciated the fact that no one else had worn them. The fact that they looked and felt more like sneakers than shoes helped.

As promised, Hope bought Carrie a hot dog and beer. It took only a few minutes for Carrie to inhale the food. Hope settled down next to her on the bench behind the ball return and watched Hope's teammates take their turns. Jerry Jenson, the first one up, bowled a spare, as did the first bowler on the opposing team. The competition was on.

Hope was the third one up. She took a deep breath and demanded her nerves to calm down. A quick glance at Carrie, who had her fingers crossed and mouthed the words "you'll do great," helped. Hope grabbed her ball and walked to the lane. Another deep breath. *Block everything else out. Look down the lane and see where you want your ball to go.* The sound of Carrie's voice in her head told her what to do. They had worked endlessly on her technique and follow-through. She wanted to make Carrie proud. Hope held her ball up, counted out four steps, and let her arm swing straight back and forward again, releasing the ball as she did. It traveled down the lane, knocking three pins down. Damn. All right. The next shot will be better. *Slow down, take your time. No need to rush it.* Carrie's words again.

She turned to wait for her ball to return and caught Carrie's eye. Carrie gave her a thumbs-up. *Carrie. Godsend Carrie.* She was so glad she had come into her life. So glad her sister had insisted she go to that damn grief support group. That was something she never thought she would say.

She aimed a little more to the left for her second roll. To her surprise, all but one of the pins went down. The team cheered as she made her way back to her seat. She tried to look nonchalant, but a huge grin broke across her face as Carrie gave her a high five.

Carrie sipped her beer as they watched the other bowlers take their turns. Carrie quietly pointed out good things the other players did as well as little errors to avoid. "See that?" Carrie said directly into Hope's ear.

The warmth of it sent a shiver down Hope's spine. She had difficulty concentrating on what Carrie was saying.

"Hope?"

"Huh?"

"Did you hear me?"

"Of course. What did you say?"

Carrie laughed. Hope warmed to the sound of it. "I asked you what he did wrong just now? How come he only knocked down two pins?"

"Oh that?" Hope scratched her head. She really hadn't been paying attention.

"Your turn, Hope," the team captain called, saving her from answering.

Her team was ahead, and Hope was determined to keep it that way. She looked intently at the pins standing at attention daring her to knock them down. She took her steps, let her arm swing like a pendulum, and released the ball. It veered slightly to the left but curved back toward the center as it rolled smoothly down the lane right toward the head pin. It hit squarely and nine pins scattered. The final pin standing was bumped by another flying by and teetered as if it was deciding whether to remain upright or fall over. The decision was made for it as another pin caught it at its base and brought it down. Hope heard the cheer from her teammates behind her before she fully realized she had just bowled her first strike—ever.

Carrie was on her feet clapping when Hope turned around, a huge smile plastered on her face. Carrie stepped forward and pulled her into a tight hug, swaying side to side.

"Great job, Hope," Carrie said as she released Hope from her arms.

"I couldn't have done that without you."

Carrie grinned wide. "I know. Aren't I great?"

"And modest too." Hope sat, grabbing Carrie's arm and pulling her down to the seat with her.

Hope was enjoying herself much more than she thought she would. It seemed she enjoyed herself no matter what she was doing as long as it involved Carrie.

It was a close game, but team Jenson Dentistry pulled it off in the end and came out ahead. Hope knew her part of the win was due to all of the help Carrie had given her. They had practiced almost every evening for the past eight days in addition to that first Sunday lesson.

"Anyone want to go get something to eat?" Jerry asked the team as they packed up their shoes and bowling balls. "My treat."

"No, thanks. We aren't really hungry," Hope said without consulting Carrie. She slipped her bowling shoes off and put her loafers back on. "Ready, Carrie?"

"Yep," Carrie answered. They said their good-byes and Carrie followed Hope out the door.

"I'm sure that hotdog wasn't enough food for you and I'm starving. Would you like to go grab a bite somewhere?" Hope asked as soon as they were in the car.

"Sure," she said. "How come you didn't want to go out with your teammates?"

"I see them all day at work. I like them, but I wanted to spend some time alone with you. Is that all right? You don't mind do you?" Hope asked.

"No, not at all. I like spending time with you, too."

"Where do you want to go? Oh, shit, I just remembered I have this stupid looking shirt on. Where can we go where I can leave my coat on?"

"It's not that bad. No one will notice." Carrie said, with a straight face that broke out into a grin.

"Liar."

"Why don't we stop at my house, seeing it's closer and you can change into one of my shirts," Carrie offered.

Hope's eyes briefly drifted down to Carrie's chest protruding a bit through her winter jacket.

Carrie noticed the glance and she felt her face get hot.

"I'm not sure I can get into your shirt," Hope said. "*Fit* into your shirt," she corrected herself as a blush spread up her neck.

"I have a few shirts I'm sure will fit you," Carrie's face still felt flushed. "Or you can just wear your bowling shirt."

"Yep. Stopping at your house."

Hope followed Carrie into her bedroom. A few of Carrie's friends had been in her bedroom before, for various reasons, but it felt a little strange having Hope standing behind her as she peered into her closet, her bed only a few feet away. *Stop it. She's a friend. Only a friend.*

"Anything strike your fancy?" Carrie asked her. She stepped out of the way so Hope could get a better look.

Hope took out a maroon pullover that looked like the material would be a little more forgiving. "How about this one?"

"Great choice," Carrie said with a smile. "Go ahead and change, I'll wait for you in the other room." Carrie went into the living room and tried to push the image of Hope removing her shirt from her mind. *What the hell is wrong with me?* She shook her head.

Carrie settled down on the couch, but she didn't have to wait long. Hope returned wearing Carrie's shirt which was definitely snug over Hope's breasts. She was at least a cup size larger than Carrie.

"Well, how does it look?" Hope did a little theatrical turn.

Hope looked incredibly sexy in her shirt. "It looks fine. Ready to go?"

"Yep."

They grabbed their coats and headed back out to Hope's car.

"Where do you want to go? Any preferences?" Hope asked.

"Anywhere is fine. How about you? Any places strike your fancy?"

"My fancy can be striked—or is it struck—by any restaurant with seafood. Are you in the mood for seafood? How about the Lobster Shack?"

"Sounds good to me."

Thirty minutes later, they were sitting at a table at the Lobster Shack waiting for their food. Hope tied a plastic bib around her neck. A cartoon outline of a big red lobster graced the front.

"You were afraid of looking ridiculous in that bowling shirt, but you have no problem with how you look in a plastic bib?"

"I am trying to keep your shirt clean. I don't want to get lobster juice or melted butter on it."

"I've seen you eat, and I've never seen you get anything on your clothes."

"You've never seen me eat seafood. It's best to sit back and not get too close. Shells and butter go everywhere." Hope gave a small chuckle. "It can be very dangerous. When the waitress comes back I'm going to ask her if they have any goggles. It might be a good idea for you to wear eye protection."

Carrie shook her head and smiled. "If it gets that bad, I'm going to ask the waitress to seat me at a different table—across the room."

"No, don't leave. All right. I'll be careful. But I'm keeping the bib on. Besides, I think it is very fashionable." She lifted the edge of the bib and glanced down at it. "And just look how sweet this little fake lobster looks on here."

"I can't argue with that. Okay, wear the bib. I'll stay. Just eat slowly and carefully."

"I promise," Hope said with a straight face, but a hint of a giggle in her voice.

The waitress came at last carrying a large tray filled with food. Hope rubbed her hands together in anticipation.

Carrie smiled and leaned back. She enjoyed watching Hope get so excited about eating. She enjoyed Hope.

CHAPTER THIRTEEN

L ove you, Gram." Carrie kissed her grandmother on the cheek. She shed a few tears on the drive to Hope's house. As much as she accepted the fact that her grandmother wasn't going to wake up, she also wasn't ready to totally let go.

As many times as Carrie and Hope had gotten together, this was the first time Carrie had been to Hope's house. An evening with a good friend, chilling out, watching a movie was just what she needed.

A quick look at the numbers on the mailbox confirmed her GPS's directions. She pulled into the driveway of Hope's large two-story house. A blast of cold air hit her in the face as soon as she opened the car door. Winter was just around the corner, and its chill was ahead of schedule. She pulled her jacket up higher around her ears to protect her from the cold wind and rang the doorbell.

Hope opened the door with the bright smile Carrie had come to expect. It seemed to warm her from the inside out. "Hey there, come in." She stepped back to let Carrie pass by her.

"I come bearing gifts." Carrie handed her a paper bag.

"Oh, what's this?" Hope asked. She took Carrie's coat and hung it up.

"Don't get too excited. It isn't much."

Hope pulled the bottle of cranberry grape juice out of the bag. "Aw, how thoughtful of you. I got you a bottle of wine."

"Great minds."

Hope laughed. "You might be giving me too much credit."

"Stop."

"I picked up a couple of movies from Redbox. Or we can pick something off of Netflix." She led the way through the living room and into the kitchen. The backsplash looked to be real stonework from the granite counter tops to the base of the natural oak cupboards. A large, but modest chandelier hung from the cathedral ceiling over a large butcher-block island with a second sink that sat in the middle of the room. A pedestal table and chairs sat off to the side near a double set of sliding glass doors opened onto a large deck. Carrie didn't know what to expect but this wasn't it. "This is a wonderful kitchen. I especially love that." She pointed to a pot rack hanging over the stove with a collection of polished stainless steel pots and pans. "That's a nice set of cookware for someone that doesn't cook."

Hope scrunched up her face. "They are kind of just for show. I usually use the same two pans all the time. They're in the cupboard by the stove. I'm really good at take-out though. Tom actually picked out this house. My tastes run a little simpler."

"I'll have to have you over for dinner more often. Get some home cooking into you."

"I would like that," Hope said with a smile that lit up her face.

Yes, I should definitely have this woman over more often.

Hope grabbed a wine glass from the cupboard. "I have red and white wine. Which would you prefer?"

Carrie raised one eyebrow with an unspoken question.

Hope seemed to read her mind. "Yes, I bought two bottles of wine for you so you could have what you wanted."

"Aw, that was so nice of you," Carrie said. "You didn't have to do that."

"I wanted to do something nice for you." She grabbed the bottle of white wine from the fridge and the bottle of red from the counter and held them up for Carrie. "Red or white?"

"I would love a glass of white."

"White it is then." She took a strange looking mechanism out of a drawer and handed it to Carrie along with the bottle. "I'll let you open this."

Hope filled a glass with ice from the dispenser on the refrigerator door and poured the juice Carrie brought into it.

Carrie struggled with the unfamiliar wine opener without much luck.

"You don't know how to use that do you?" Hope smiled.

Carrie shook her head. "Nope. I've never seen anything like this before. I'm assuming that the corkscrew part goes into the cork, but I don't see how to do that." She attempted to hand her the opener.

"Oh no," Hope said. "I'm not going to do it. You get to learn how to do it. Pull those little things that look like rabbit ears apart. Set the corkscrew thing on the top of the bottle and pull down that lever."

Carrie attempted to follow Hope's instruction, but it still wasn't working. She was starting to feel like an idiot.

Hope reached over and covered Carrie's hands with her own. Carrie immediately felt the warmth and softness. The warmth spread quickly through Carrie's body. It turned to heat as it hit her face and traveled down to her belly and below. She fought the impulse to pull her hands away. Reminding herself she shouldn't be having these feelings toward Hope.

The cork slid smoothly out of the bottleneck, with a slight popping sound as Hope's hands controlled Carrie's.

"There you go," Hope said. "Isn't that a neat little device?"

Carrie cleared her throat. "It is." She poured the wine into her glass and took a large gulp. Then another.

The feeling of Hope's touch was still on her mind when they made their way into the living room, with their drinks. Hope sat on the leather couch and patted the spot next to her for Carrie. There was a fresh bowl of popcorn sitting on the coffee table in front of them.

"I thought you didn't cook," Carrie said, breaking the momentary silence.

"Oh, I cook microwave popcorn. In fact, that is my specialty." Hope smiled that smile again.

Carrie couldn't help but smile back. She took a sip of her wine. "Mmm, this is good."

"I'm glad you like it." Hope pulled her bare feet under herself and turned to face Carrie. "So, how was your day?"

"Fine, mostly paperwork today, so not too exciting. How about you? Anything exciting?"

"Every day is exciting where I work. I cleaned teeth and then cleaned some more teeth. And oh yeah, did I mention I cleaned teeth?"

"I believe you did."

"Actually, this is the most exciting part of my day."

"Your day must be pretty boring if I'm the highlight."

"You *are* the highlight for sure. I really enjoy your company. I mean that." Hope had a way of making Carrie feel good about herself. That was one of the things Carrie liked best about her.

"Ditto, my friend." Carrie raised her glass and Hope clinked her glass against it. "What movies did you get?"

Hope handed her the two DVDs that sat next to the bowl of popcorn. "Here you go, take a look.

Carrie set her wine down to look. Both DVDs were recent releases.

"Did you have a favorite?" Carrie asked.

"Nope. Either is fine with me. Your choice."

Carrie made her selection and Hope loaded it into the DVD player and turned down the lights.

Carrie found herself only half watching the movie as her mind returned again and again to Hope, sitting next to her. Their hands touched more than once as they reached into the shared bowl of popcorn.

"Sorry," she said the third time it happened. If Hope noticed or heard her, she didn't respond.

"What did you think?" Hope asked Carrie as the credits rolled. The bowl of popcorn was empty as were the glasses they had long since abandoned. Hope turned on the small lamp on the side table.

I think you look beautiful in this light. "It was good." She said, hoping Hope wouldn't ask any specific questions. She was sure she wouldn't be able to answer them.

"You okay?"

"Yes, I'm fine. Why are you asking?"

"You just seemed far away for a minute."

"Sorry. I guess I'm a little tired." The light picked up the gold flakes in Hope's eyes making them almost glow.

"I'll bet you are, with work and visiting your grandmother and being kind enough to teach me to bowl." Hope reached over and rubbed Carrie's arm. "I really appreciate that by the way. You made a big difference. I would have bowled nothing but gutter balls if it weren't for you."

Carrie stopped hearing the words as soon as Hope touched her. She struggled to ignore the electric sensation coursing through her arm.

"Yes." Carrie said, trying to figure out the conversation.

"Yes what?" Hope asked, looking a little confused.

"Yes, ma'am?"

"Very funny. Never mind. Just know I appreciate all the help and time you put into it." She pulled her hand away.

Carrie felt the loss of it immediately and fought the urge to reach out for Hope's hand again. *Straight. Friend. Modeling for you. Straight.* "Of course. Anything for you." She still wasn't sure what they were talking about. "I really should get going. I know you have to work in the morning. I guess I do too." She stood.

"I really had a nice time," she said, walking to the door. "Thank you so much for the wine."

"Thanks so much for coming and the juice." Hope handed Carrie her coat. Carrie slipped it on and Hope gave her a tight hug. "I'll see you Saturday for modeling, right?"

"Yes. I'm sure we'll talk before then. Thanks again." The frigid air did little to squelch the heat that was building inside her. She turned before slipping into the driver's seat and waved at Hope who was standing in the doorway, with her arms wrapped tightly around her in the cold. Hope waved back but didn't go inside until Carrie drove away. Carrie could see her in the rearview mirror.

"I've got to figure this out before I say or do something stupid," she said to herself. The last thing she wanted to do was lose Hope by scaring her off.

❖

Hope brought the empty popcorn bowl and glasses into the kitchen and left them on the counter. She turned off the lights on her way upstairs. Once in her room she undressed slowly as she thought about the evening and how much she enjoyed spending time with Carrie. Her favorite thing about Carrie was the way they could laugh together, even at the silly things. She loved to laugh, but there hadn't been a lot of people in her life she had that connection with. But her connection with Carrie was deeper than just that. It was the rare connection Hope had been missing in her life. She hadn't had a connection like that since college. College. So long ago. She didn't want to think about it, or anything that had happened there. She pushed her thoughts aside as she slipped her nightgown over her head. She wasn't going to let her thoughts go in that direction. She had pushed all of that to the back of her mind a long time ago and that was where it was going to stay. Now was not the time to be reliving it.

CHAPTER FOURTEEN

Carrie arrived at Sunnyside Nursing Home a little earlier than usual. She just couldn't keep her mind on work. She walked down the brightly lit hallway to her grandmother's room.

"Hello, Carrie." Marge greeted her with her usual chipper attitude. "We are just finishing up a sponge bath." The aide put a towel onto the cart in front of her. "There we go. All set, Mrs. Brice." She patted Gram's hand. "I'll see you later." She wheeled the cart toward the door.

"Thank you," Carrie said to her.

"Enjoy your visit." Marge left the room, closing the door behind her. Carrie took a seat in her usual spot next to the bed. She sat for a long time without talking, absorbing her grandmother's features. She looked so different, yet completely the same. It was so confusing. As was another aspect of her life.

"Hi, Gram." She cleared her throat. "I need to talk to you. Got a little time to listen?" Carrie closed her eyes for a few seconds and rubbed a hand over her face. She took a deep breath. "Okay, Gram, here's the deal. I have feelings for someone who—well—who I probably shouldn't be having feelings for. I know if you could answer me your first question would be 'Why, what's the matter with her?' Oh, Gram, I can just hear you saying that to me." Carrie wiped at the tears forming in the corner of her eyes. "This conversation sure would be easier if I didn't have to carry both ends of it." She smiled a sad smile at her grandmother.

"There isn't anything wrong with her, that's just it. I think she's perfect. Did you hear me, Gram?" Carrie paused as if waiting for an answer. "It's Hope, Gram. Remember I told you about meeting her at that support group? Well, I knew I liked her, but turns out the more time I spend with her, the more I realize it is so much more than *like*. But here's the problem, Gram, she's straight. Been married with a kid and everything. The whole nine yards. The straightest of straights. I also hired her as my model for a couple of paintings. So, hitting on her would just be wrong. Of course, I haven't told her about my feelings. Because, well, because it just isn't the thing you do. You don't just go around telling a straight woman you have feelings for her. It tends to scare them away. So, I'm not going to tell her. I am just going to feel these feelings for her and love being with her and be the best friend I can be. I want to keep her in my life, and I don't want to make her uncomfortable or not want to be around me."

Carrie went to the window. The sun was already starting to go down. *I hate daylight savings time. It gets dark way too early now.* She watched the last of the leaves fly through the air and scatter across the ground. She knew the snow would soon replace them. A chill went through her at the thought.

Without her consent, her mind replaced the barren winter scene in her head with an entirely different one. She saw herself and Hope walking hand in hand as the snow fell around them and the sun shone bright above. She shook the thoughts away.

"Gram," she said, turning back to her. "What would you say if you could hear me and answer me? Would you tell me it's wrong to feel this way or would you tell me that it's okay? You've always been so accepting of me and I love you for that. But this is someone I just can't have. I don't know what to do with all these feelings."

Carrie sat again and picked up the tube of hand lotion and proceeded to massage it into her grandmother's skin. "I just feel so good when I'm with her. You know what I mean? You always told me Grandpa was your true love. You said you knew you would love him from the first time you saw him. That's how I feel about Hope. She isn't like anyone I have ever met before. I get all excited when I know I'm going to be seeing her. If we happen to touch it's like—well, it's like nothing I've felt before." Carrie laughed at herself. "Probably too much information, huh?" Carrie laughed at herself. "Okay, I won't give you any more details. But I can't help feeling what I'm feeling. I just want to be around her all the time." Carrie gently worked the lotion in. "So, I'm going to be around her and that's it. I just have to ignore all these feelings I'm having. I think I can do it. She doesn't have to know what's going on in my head." Carrie finished one hand and started with the lotion on the second one.

"I've thought about not hanging out with her any more. You know, just putting some distance between us. But I can't do that. I can't stop seeing her. I want her in my life. So, that's that. She's in my life and she's my friend. That has to be enough for me." Carrie put her face in her hands. "Shit. What am I going to do with all these feelings?"

CHAPTER FIFTEEN

Carrie answered the phone on the second ring. "Hi, Hope," she said. She had just gotten home from work.

"Hey there. I was wondering if it would be okay if we changed the schedule for tomorrow a little. Would it be all right if I came over at one o'clock to model instead of at eleven? I can stay as late as you want me to."

How about staying all night? Oh my God, what is wrong with me? Stop it! "Sure, that would be fine. What's up?" She took off her coat and flung it over the arm of the couch.

"My sister asked me to watch her twins tomorrow morning for a little while. I'm still trying to figure out what to do to entertain them. They're seven and I don't have any of Derrick's old toys any more. I would let them play his video games, but my sister would kill me for exposing them to violence. He doesn't have anything nice and peaceful."

"Why don't you take them sledding at Harris Park? It should be great with all the snow we got last night. It's supposed to be a nice sunny day."

"Hmm, that's a good idea. Could I possibly interest you in joining us? I hear it's supposed to be a nice sunny day tomorrow."

"Yeah, you just heard that from me." Carrie laughed.

"Oh yeah, that's where I heard it." Hope chuckled. "So, what do you think? Could you stand being with me and two little boys for a few hours?"

Carrie opened the fridge and pulled out a beer. "I think I can stand being around the boys. It's you I'm wondering about."

"Ha, ha. Very funny."

"Sure, I'll go with you. What time are you thinking of going?"

"Great! How about I pick you up at nine thirty and then we can go get the boys. I'll double-check with Marcy to make sure they have a sled, and that it's something they would like to do."

"Okay, let me know for sure if that's the plan. I'll start looking for my boots. I haven't worn them since last winter."

"You got it. I'll call you later tonight and let you know. Thanks, Carrie."

"Anytime. Talk to you later. Bye."

"Bye," Hope said softly. The word was spoken barely above a whisper, but it affected Carrie and shot a rush through her, causing her skin to feel warm. Carrie wasn't sure if she should enjoy the feelings Hope stirred in her or push them away. The only thing she knew for sure was that she had never felt like this about anyone before.

Carrie was dressed warmly in her thickest winter jacket, scarf, gloves, and boots when Hope picked her up the next day. It was bright and sunny, just as the weatherman had predicted. They chatted away as Hope drove to her sister's house.

"I really appreciate you coming with us today," Hope told her.

"I'm very glad you asked me." She liked being included in Hope's life.

"I'll be right back," Hope said. She put the car in park in front of her sister's house. "The boys are supposed to be ready, so this should be quick."

As promised, Hope was back with her nephews in a matter of minutes. Hope introduced the boys to Carrie. They seemed excited to have her along. The four of them headed to Harris Park, two brightly colored sleds tucked into the trunk.

They walked carefully across the slick snow from the car to the hill, just a few yards from the parking lot. The snow crunched under their feet, a thin layer of ice covered it. The boys dragged their sleds behind them. There wasn't anyone else on the hill yet, although Carrie was sure it would soon be full of sledding children.

Hope helped Richie onto his sled. She had explained to Carrie that Richie had his mother's light brown eyes and his father's dark blond hair, which was now covered by a bright green knit hat. A matching scarf was wrapped around his neck and tucked into the front of his blue snowsuit. Rubber boots with zippers up the side, protected his feet. Hope was about to give him a push down the hill when he called out for his brother. "We want to go together," he told Hope.

"Okay," she said. She held the back of the long orange plastic sled while Mark climbed on. Mark's looks were very different from his brother's, making it obvious they weren't identical twins. He had brown eyes like his brother, but they were much darker, as were his hair and thick eyelashes. His hair had a slight curl to it, whereas Richie's was straight as a pin. They wore matching snowsuits and boots, but his hat and scarf were bright red. Mark clung tightly to his brother's back and Hope pushed the sled sending them sliding down the hill. The boys laughed and giggled as they flew over the packed snow to the bottom, two hundred feet away. Hope and Carrie cheered them on.

Both boys jumped off the sled at the bottom of the hill. Mark grabbed the rope tied to the front of the sled and started back up. He had only taken about ten steps when he slipped and fell. He lost his grip on the rope and the sled slid back down the hill.

Carrie and Hope watched as he got back on his feet and went to retrieve the sled.

Richie laughed as his brother picked up the rope and once again started up the hill, only to slip again. "Watch me," Richie said to him as he grabbed the rope. "Do it like this." He started up the hill, stomping his feet hard into the snow. He got a little farther than his brother had when his feet went out from under him, and he and his sled went sliding down. Both boys were laughing hysterically.

"Try coming up slower," Hope called to her nephews.

They both tried again, Mark pulling the sled behind him. Both boys ended up falling and sliding down the hill again.

As soon as Hope caught Carrie's eye they both broke out laughing.

"Try it one more time," Carrie yelled. They tried again with the same results.

"We can't do it," Mark yelled. "We need help."

"What should we do?" Carrie asked Hope.

Hope shrugged. She noticed the other sled lying on the snow behind Carrie. "Should we go and get them?" She pointed at the sled.

"What?" Carrie asked.

"Should we get on that sled and slide it down there and help them up?"

"I haven't been on a sled in twenty years," Carrie said.

"Me either, but I don't feel like trying to walk down there and end up sliding on my ass, so I'm thinking sledding down would be a better idea. Are you game?" She smiled. Carrie could see a bit of childlike abandon in the smile.

"Sure," Carrie laughed. "Why not." She pulled the sled over and positioned it so it faced down the hill.

"Move over to the side," Hope called to the twins and she waved her arm over to the right.

The boys half walked and half crawled over to the side and out of the way.

Hope sat on the front of the long sled and held onto the rope. She scooted her butt as far forward as she could go, her legs folded underneath her. She turned to Carrie and patted the space behind her.

"Are you sure about this?"

"Of course I'm not. Come on, let's go for a wild ride." Hope patted the spot again. Carrie sat. It was a tight fit with her legs on the edge of the sled on both sides of Hope. She wrapped her arms around Hope's waist.

"This is crazy," Carrie said, feeling both elated and a little scared. She wasn't afraid of going down the hill or getting hurt. She was scared of being so close to Hope.

Hope used her hands to move them forward over the snow until the sled started to move on its own. The slick ice-covered snow and the weight of them on the sled sent it screaming down the hill at a high rate of speed. They flew by the boys and continued another twenty feet farther. Without warning, they hit a bump and they both went flying into the air. The sled flew out from under them, and they ended up in a heap with Carrie on top of Hope. She looked into Hope's eyes and burst out laughing. Hope joined in.

"Are you all right?" Hope asked, looking up at Carrie.

It took all the strength Carrie could muster to resist the urge to lean down and kiss her. They were so close. Carrie could feel Hope's breath on her face. She felt Hope's body under hers. All she could do was nod.

The boys came running over to them, slipping and sliding on the way. Carrie turned her head to look up into their surprised, little faces. She realized she was still lying on top of Hope. There was no graceful way of moving off of her. She rolled sideways until she was lying flat on her back on the snow.

Hope sat up. "Are you sure you're all right?" she asked Carrie again.

"Yep," Carrie said, still on her back. "Are you?" She dared a look at Hope.

"I think so," she looked at her nephews. "I guess the snow is pretty slippery, huh?" They giggled at her. Both boys grabbed one of Carrie's hands and pulled her into a sitting position.

Once they were on their feet they started slowly and carefully up the hill. Each held the hand of a twin and dragged a sled behind them.

"We want to go again," Mark yelled when they got to the top.

"I don't think that is a good idea," Hope told him. "But I do have another thought. I think we should all go to the Duchess Diner and have a nice cup of hot chocolate with lots and lots of whipped cream on top. What would you think about that?"

"Yeah!" both boys and Carrie said in unison.

"It's unanimous then. Hot chocolate, here we come."

Carrie followed them back to the car, doing her best to keep her eyes off of Hope's snow covered rear end and wondering if she should tell Hope that she should wipe it off or do it for her.

Carrie had a cup of tea poured and ready for her on the coffee table when Hope came into the living room after putting her clothes back on. Carrie had finished the first painting, and this was their third session for the second one. Carrie had said one more modeling session and they should be all done. She hadn't let Hope see them yet, but Carrie said she was very pleased with the way they were coming out.

Hope was going to miss sitting half naked across from Carrie, chatting while Carrie painted. She laughed at how silly that sounded in her head.

"Dressed already?" Carrie asked. "You're fast."

Hope plopped down on the couch next to her and set her shoes on the floor. "Well, don't let it get around, it will ruin my reputation."

"You're so funny." Carrie laughed. "How come you're so funny?" Carrie's wide smile relaxed into a grin.

"Insecurity."

"What? Seriously?"

"Yes, I think I discovered early on I could win people over with humor. I felt like people would like me if I could make them laugh."

"You make me laugh all the time. Are you insecure with me?"

"No." Hope hesitated. "Actually, I feel very secure with you."

"Then how come you're always making me laugh?"

Hope thought about it for a moment before answering. "Because I love the sound of your laugh, and I love your smile."

Carrie blushed and sipped her tea. In an attempt to cover it, Hope suspected.

"How is Derrick doing? He should be home for Thanksgiving soon, shouldn't he?"

"I talked to him yesterday. He'll be home on Monday. He's bringing Erin with him, so I guess they're still together." Hope hesitated. "This is the first major holiday since his father died. I am not sure how he is going to handle it. He had a really hard time when Tom died."

"I'm sure it was hard on both of you."

"I'll be okay. It's just hard watching my son go through it. This might sound terrible, but for the first time since my husband died, I finally feel like I can breathe. He was sick for so long and I felt like I couldn't catch my breath. I felt like I was waiting for him to die."

"No, it doesn't sound terrible. I know exactly what you're saying." Carrie gave her a reassuring look.

"I was married to the man for a long time and I shouldn't have been with him at all."

"Why did you stay?"

"I wanted to give it time at the beginning. I was waiting for it to feel right. Money was so tight. We had a baby, I had a part-time minimum wage job. There was no way I could afford to take care of myself, let alone a baby. I really didn't want to go running back to Mom and Dad. So, I stayed."

"Do you feel like all those years you were wasting your life?" Carrie asked quietly.

"No. I felt like I was wasting his life."

Carrie set her teacup down. "What do you mean?"

"The first few years of our marriage were tough, especially financially. Tom was still going to school and working part-time. I was a new mother and I was working part-time, but when I wasn't working, I was home with this baby I adored. Being a parent is such a tough job, but Derrick was such a good baby and a good kid." She took a deep breath and continued. "Tom got a great job as soon as he graduated. He was a good husband and a great father. He was home with us after work. He was there for little league games and school plays. He remembered birthdays and anniversaries."

"Then why are you saying you wasted his life?" Carrie asked.

"Because a good man like that deserved a wife who loved him. I couldn't do that for him. I couldn't love him," Hope sighed at the old memories and at the relief she felt in finally letting them out. She had kept it inside for so long she felt like a weight was lifted from her soul as she released it.

"I raised his son, I sat across from him at dinner, I let him make love to me, but I couldn't love him. Believe me, I tried." She brushed away the tears that began to escape from her eyes.

"Oh, Hope," Carrie said. She pulled several tissues from the box on the table beside her and used one to gently wipe the tears from Hope's cheek. She handed the rest of the tissues to her. "I know there is nothing I can say to make you feel any better about this, but I think you are an extraordinary person. I think Tom was very lucky to have you."

"I shouldn't have been with Tom in the first place. I went to him out of fear. Well, not exactly fear. Confusion. I don't know. But it wasn't out of love. That wasn't fair to him."

"Was it horrible for you? Having to pretend like that? Having him make love to you when you didn't feel it?" Carrie asked, the concern showing in her voice.

Hope was grateful Carrie didn't ask for more of an explanation. "It wasn't horrible. But it wasn't good either. It was sort of like getting vanilla all the time when all you really wanted was chocolate." Hope laughed through the tears. "Leave it to me to make an analogy using food."

Carrie wrapped her arms around Hope. She wanted nothing more than to comfort her. To help her let go of the guilt and regret. She pulled Hope in close. She could feel Hope's tears as she pressed her cheek against Hope's cheek. She could feel Hope's heart beating in her chest and Hope's breath, warm on her neck.

Before she knew what she was doing, and without any real thought Carrie tilted her head and brought her lips to Hope's mouth. She kissed her tenderly at first and then with more urgency as she felt Hope respond to her.

Hope's tongue entered her mouth and searched out her own. Carrie trembled with the electricity that coursed through her. She had never felt such excitement from a kiss. She moved her hands up Hope's back and into her hair. Carrie pushed her body forward into Hope and felt their breasts press together.

As suddenly as the kiss started, Hope pulled back, stopping it.

The look on her face told Carrie everything she needed to know. "I'm so sorry. Hope I…"

Hope struggled out of Carrie's embrace.

"Oh my God, Hope." Carrie had trouble speaking. Her breath came in gasps. "I am so sorry. That was so inappropriate of me. I am so sorry."

Hope stood. "I need to go." She slipped her feet into her shoes without looking at Carrie.

"Please don't go, Hope," Carrie tried to keep her voice even. She felt tears start to well up in her eyes. "Please don't go," she repeated. "I just…I'm sorry. I just care about you and…" The words of explanation weren't coming. She wanted to explain but realized she couldn't adequately voice it without telling Hope her true feelings. She was so afraid of scaring Hope away. She didn't want to lose her friend. She thought she had done just that with her stupid thoughtless behavior.

"I just need to go." Hope walked to the door, stopping just long enough to get her coat. Carrie followed close behind her, stammering her apologies. Hope left without looking back, closing the door behind her.

Carrie stared at the door. She couldn't believe what had just happened. She had let her feelings come to the surface, and she had offended or scared Hope. Probably both. She reached out and grabbed the doorknob considering whether to open it and call out to Hope or not. Beg her to come back so she could explain. But she knew she couldn't explain away her feelings. She thought it would only send Hope further away.

She turned her back to the door and leaned against it as the tears began to flow freely. She slid slowly down the door until she was sitting on the floor sobbing. *Stupid, stupid, stupid. Why did I do that? Why couldn't I just love her and hide my feelings from her? Now I've lost her. I've lost her.*

❖

Hope started her car and backed it out of Carrie's driveway. *I can't go through this again.* She put the car in drive and pulled out onto the street. She drove without any awareness of where she was going. She just knew she needed to get away. She couldn't be in the same space as Carrie. She knew it was dangerous. Her body had reacted to Carrie's kiss. She couldn't let that happen. She couldn't let anything happen with Carrie like it had with Maria so many years ago.

Maria had been a mistake. Maria was the reason she slept with Tom. The reason she got pregnant with Derrick. The reason she spent years with a man she didn't love. And now Carrie was bringing back all of the feelings she had had with Maria. *All of the feelings of... of what... of what?* Her brain screamed the question. *Of love. She is bringing back all of the feelings of love.*

Hope pulled the car over to the side of the road. She loved Carrie. She was running because she loved Carrie, just like she had run all those years ago because she had loved Maria.

Hope thought back to Maria. She hadn't allowed her mind to go there fully for many years. She met Maria the day she moved into her dorm at college. Maria was tall and thin with long, thick Auburn hair and a quick smile. Her hazel eyes were heavy with thick dark lashes. Maria's room was across the hall from Hope's and they shared several classes together. They enjoyed each other's company and became quick friends.

Hope felt energized and alive when she was with Maria. She looked forward to their classes together. Their friendship spilled over into other aspects of Hope's life. They studied together, went to parties and movies, and laughed. A lot.

Maria and Hope often rented movies from the DVD shop in town and watched them on the small television Hope had brought from home. It wasn't unusual for them to watch from the comfort of Hope's bed. It seemed so natural to cuddle together as the movie played.

Hope's roommate went home most weekends, leaving Hope with the room to herself. Maria often slept over on those weekends. Sometimes in her roommate's bed and sometimes in Hope's.

Hope thought back to the final weekend they were alone watching a movie in Hope's bed. Maria leaned over and kissed Hope lightly on the neck as she nuzzled into her. Before she realized what was happening, they were kissing. Hands and lips were everywhere. Hope felt more alive than she had ever felt in her life.

It didn't take long for their clothes to be discarded. They made love with an urgency and passion Hope had never felt before. They slept through the night in the comfort of each other's arms. But when the daylight broke through the window the next morning, Maria was gone.

It wasn't until several days later when Hope finally caught up with her after class that Maria finally talked to her. She had avoided Hope's phone calls and even her own dorm room in an attempt to avoid Hope.

She said she didn't want to deal with what it meant to love a woman. She didn't want to be gay. She didn't want people to hate her. She didn't want her parents to know, to be mad at her. She didn't want any of what it meant. So, she ran. She broke Hope's heart. Into. A. Million. Pieces. Hope didn't think she would ever be able to put those pieces back together.

Then along came Tom. Tom who liked her. Tom who soon said he loved her. Tom who she slept with to try to forget about the woman she loved.

He was good-looking, tall and muscular, with curly dark hair and baby blue eyes. She felt no sparks with him, but that didn't matter in the moment. She just wanted to feel wanted. And Tom wanted her. Derrick was conceived by mistake, and her life changed forever.

She had run from her pain, just like she ran from Carrie. She ran because she feared feeling that pain again. She ran because she had feelings for Carrie that she didn't want to admit. To herself. Or to Carrie. She was running from the possibility of love.

Her heart pounded in her chest and her skin was on fire. It was Carrie. She squeezed her eyes shut. She tried to squeeze the feeling away. But it was no use. She couldn't squeeze Carrie out of her. She couldn't make the feelings go away. What was she going to do with this? What was she going to do with Carrie?

What if I stop running? What if I just take a chance? Maybe it *was* time to stop running. Maybe it was time to let the possibility of love into her life. But she wasn't sure what Carrie felt for her. Did Carrie have feelings too or was she just feeling sorry for her in the moment? What if she went back and Carrie didn't feel the same way she did? What if she lost Carrie the way she lost Maria?

Oh. But what if she didn't?

She put the car in gear and pulled back onto the road and did a U-turn heading back to Carrie's house. She just hoped she hadn't totally blown it with Carrie. She hoped Carrie would forgive her for running away. She hoped maybe, just maybe, Carrie had feelings for her too.

❖

Carrie felt like she had cried all the tears from her body. She stood, using the door for support. She walked to the bathroom and turned on the shower, undressing as the water heated up.

She kicked her clothes off to the side and stepped under the hot spray. She willed the water to wash away her pain. The last remnants of her tears were washed down the shower drain.

The sound of the doorbell broke through the rhythmic sound of water hitting the tiled walls. Carrie wasn't sure she could trust her ears. She turned off the water and listened, standing still and squinting her eyes as if that would make her hearing more acute. She heard it again. It was definitely the doorbell.

Hope? No, it isn't Hope. Hope isn't coming back. You'll be lucky if you ever see her again. You really messed up with that one. Without further thought, Carrie stepped out of the shower. She grabbed her bathrobe from the hook on the back of the bathroom door. The robe soaked up most of the water on her naked skin. She tied the belt around her waist as she half walked, half ran to the door.

Carrie reached for the doorknob, but hesitated, not sure she should open it. She was still trying to decide when the sound of the doorbell rang again, startling her. Without further thought, she flung the door open and found herself looking directly into Hope's eyes.

Chapter Sixteen

Carrie opened her mouth to speak. "Hope, I am so sor—" But her words were cut off by the kiss Hope crushed into her mouth. Hope wrapped an arm around Carrie's waist and pulled her in close with a sharp tug. Carrie melted into the kiss. She felt Hope's tongue pushing gently at her lips until they parted, letting Hope in. After having her way with Carrie's mouth, Hope's lips traveled down to her neck, kissing and nibbling their way, leaving a hot, moist trail. Carrie tilted her head back, giving Hope full access.

Hope slipped her hand into the robe at Carrie's shoulder and pushed it back, exposing the tender skin of Carrie's shoulder. She ran her tongue along the dip in the flesh above her collarbone.

Carrie trembled as Hope's tongue traveled from her throat back up to her lips. Hope pulled back from the kiss. Carrie felt the sudden loss of her lips. She opened her eyes.

"Carrie, I am so sorry for running. Please forgive me and let me explain."

Carrie wasn't sure she could speak. Her breath was rapid, and her heart threatened to leap out of her chest. She nodded.

Hope took her hand and led her to the living room. She eased Carrie down on the couch and sat next to her. She brought Carrie's hand to her lips and kissed it. She held it tight as she looked directly into Carrie's eyes. Hope brushed away a strand of wet hair from Carrie's face.

"There's something I didn't tell you about myself." She blinked a few times. Carrie suspected she was trying to keep the tears at bay. "It was when I was in college. I fell in love with someone. It wasn't Tom. It was a woman. We started out as friends and ended up sleeping together." She paused.

Carrie tried to take it all in. *Was Hope saying she was a lesbian? Was she saying she slept with a woman and didn't like it?* That kiss didn't seem like she wouldn't like it.

Carrie brushed a tear away as it rolled down Hope's cheek. "She ran. She broke my heart. And I ran, Carrie. I ran to Tom and that is how I ended up pregnant. I didn't love him. I didn't have any real feelings for him at all, but I knew he liked me, and I used him to prove to myself I was worth something. Worth being loved."

"Oh, Hope."

"Fear is a great motivator. I feared I wasn't good enough. Fear motivated me into Tom's bed, into motherhood, and into marriage. I put all of that fear and all of the feelings I had for Maria out of my mind as if they didn't exist." Hope swallowed and closed her eyes as the memories and emotions seemed to flood over her. "When you kissed me, it brought all of those feelings back."

"I am so sorry, Hope. I had no idea. I didn't mean to do anything that would be painful for you. I—I—I just feel, well, I feel so…" Carrie was struggling with the words.

"Don't apologize, Carrie. I'm feeling it, too. You were just brave enough to act on it. I was the coward who ran. But, Carrie, I'm not running any more. So if you still want me, I'm here. I'm here and not going anywhere. So, what do you think? Any chance you want me?"

"Oh my God, yes." Carrie pulled her in and hugged her tightly, almost afraid to let go. She pulled back just enough to look into Hope's eyes.

"So where do we go from here?" Carrie searched Hope's face for the answer. She didn't have to wait long.

Hope whispered. "To your bedroom?" She raised her eyebrows.

Without another word, Carrie stood and put her hand out for Hope. Hope took it and allowed her to lead the way.

Carrie turned and pulled Hope into a kiss. Without losing contact, Hope untied the belt around Carrie's waist and slipped her hands inside. She let out a low groan and Carrie felt a surge of moisture from her touch.

Hope took a couple of steps back. Carrie watched as Hope's eyes swept over her body causing a rush of heat to surge through her.

A single word escaped Hope's mouth at the sight. "Beautiful," she said. She slowly unbuttoned her own shirt and let it fall to the floor. Her bra quickly followed.

She stepped back into Carrie's waiting arms. Carrie felt Hope's nipples harden as they pressed against her own. She struggled to pull the snap open on Hope's jeans. And reached for the zipper as soon as the snap relented. Hope kicked out of her shoes.

Carrie pulled the zipper down slowly and slipped her fingers inside the gaping denim and ran them over the silky material of Hope's underwear. Hope let out a small gasp. Carrie could feel the moisture through the cloth.

Hope pushed her pants down, taking her panties with them. They hung at her ankles for a moment before she stepped out of them.

The only thing that stood in the way of them being totally naked was the opened robe. Hope slipped her hands in between the material and Carrie's shoulders and pushed the robe off of her. It joined the rest of the discarded clothes on the floor.

Hope stared into Carrie's green eyes as she eased her backward until Carrie was lying on her back on the bed. She wasted no time pulling Hope down on top of her.

Carrie's hands settled on Hope's rear, squeezing the flesh and pulling her in closer as Carrie spread her legs allowing Hope to settle in between them. Their lips merged in a deep kiss, causing Hope to tremble with hot desire.

Hope consciously slowed her kisses. "I don't want to rush this," she whispered. "I want to savor making love to you." She ran her hands through Carrie's hair.

Carrie wrapped her legs around Hope's, opening them wider creating more contact between Hope's wetness and her own. She rocked her pelvis against Hope sending a wave of delicious sensations through her resulting in a low groan. Carrie's kiss caught the sound before it escaped into the air.

Carrie's breath came in ragged gasps as Hope's pelvic movements began to match her own. Carrie's fingers held on tightly digging into the flesh on Hope's backside.

Hope traced a wet trail down Carrie's neck with her tongue. She pushed herself up creating space between their bodies, so she could work her way farther down Carrie's body with her mouth. She rolled off Carrie to gain better access to Carrie's breasts and ran her tongue across each breast stopping to suck a hardened nipple into her mouth.

She ran her fingers through Carrie's slick wetness and she entered her.

"I love how wet you are," Hope whispered. She moved her fingers rhythmically as Carrie's hips rose to meet them and her heels dug in the mattress. Carrie's hips lifted off the bed as her breath quickened and held completely as an orgasm ripped through her.

Hope slowed her movement as she felt Carrie's body react and tighten around her fingers. She continued to bathe Carrie's nipples with her tongue. Carrie wrapped her arms around Hope, holding on tight as if she was trying to keep from rising off the bed.

Hope gently removed her fingers as Carrie came down from the crest. Carrie lifted Hope's head from her breast and brought it to her face. She kissed her passionately, plunging her tongue into Hope's mouth.

"Wow," was all Carrie said, as she pulled her mouth from Hope's.

"Wow," Hope repeated. She wrapped her arms around Carrie and held her tight. How could she have ever run from this woman?

Carrie's breathing slowly returned to normal. Hope raked the back of her fingernails across Carrie's stomach and chest as she lay quietly in the comfort of Carrie's arms.

Carrie planted small, lingering kisses on Hope's neck as she moved her hands over Hope's body. Hope's nipple hardened under her touch and Hope sucked in a breath as Carrie moved her fingers downward and she slipped them through the wet folds. Hope shuddered as Carrie entered her.

"Okay?"

Hope had trouble speaking. "Oh my God, yes. This is perfect. You are perfect."

Carrie increased the pressure from her fingers as Hope's body reacted to her touch. Her mouth found Hope's mouth again, swallowing the small sounds of pleasure escaping Hope's throat.

Hope arched her back as she found her release in Carrie's arms, letting out a small cry.

Carrie held her tight until Hope's body relaxed and they settled into each other.

"You are my chocolate," Hope whispered.

Carrie planted a soft kiss on Hope's lips. "I'm so glad."

They fell asleep in each other's arms and stayed that way until the morning light.

CHAPTER SEVENTEEN

G ood morning," Carrie said as soon as Hope opened her eyes. Carrie had been taking great pleasure in watching her sleep. "How ya doing?"

Hope pulled Carrie into a deep kiss. "What does that tell you?"

"I'm thinking you're doing okay." Carrie kissed Hope on the nose.

"Can I ask you something?"

"You can ask me anything." Carrie waited patiently while Hope seemed to gather her thoughts.

"You've done this before—been with other women. You know, other than Tom, the only other person I've been with was Maria. And that was only once. Was this okay for you?" She paused. "Was I okay for you?"

Carrie couldn't help but smile. "Yes, I've been with other women. But last night was so different for me. Being with *you* was so different for me." She looked into Hope's eyes trying to read her thoughts. "Yes. You were more than just okay for me. It was wonderful."

Hope was quiet for several long moments.

"What are you thinking?" Carrie asked.

Hope pushed a strand of hair out of Carrie's face and tucked it behind her ear. "I was just thinking how last night you showed me who I've always been." She held Carrie's face between her hands and kissed her again. "It was very special for me too, Carrie. I care about you so much."

Carrie sucked in a breath as Hope began to explore her body.

"I am amazed at how my body reacts to touching you. The feel of your breast, the soft flesh and the hard nipple. Just touching you is making me wet."

"Ooh, let me see." Carrie reached between Hope's legs. "Oh my God, you're right. Keep touching me and let's see just how wet you can get. I'll keep checking on your progress." Carrie moved her fingers over Hope's swollen flesh.

Hope's moans resonated from deep in her throat.

"I think I need to check this out closer," Carrie said. "What do you think, Hope, should I check it out a little closer?"

Hope's voice broke as she attempted to answer. She finally managed to squeak out a "yes."

Carrie wasted no time in moving down Hope's body, planting wet kisses along the way. Goose bumps erupted as she circled her tongue around Hope's belly button. Carrie's kisses skipped over the place her fingers had found earlier. She lifted Hope's legs up slightly off the bed and planted kisses on her inner thighs. Hope's legs began to tremble as Carrie continued to tease her.

Carrie ran her hands over the smooth skin of Hope's hips and down her outer thighs. Her mouth was inches from Hope's sweet spot, and she let out a hot breath followed by a quick flick of her tongue, causing Hope to moan. Carrie felt Hope's hands on her head trying to push her down, but Carrie wasn't done with her teasing. She tenderly licked the inside of Hope's thigh, moving farther away from the spot Hope so desperately tried to direct her to.

Without warning, Carrie moved forward and plunged her tongue into Hope's wetness. Hope let out a cry of pleasure. She pulled her fingers through Carrie's hair.

Hope's hips rose to meet Carrie's mouth. Their bodies became one and moved in unison. Carrie slipped her hands under Hope's butt. She held tight and pulled Hope in closer to her face and held her there as she let her tongue continue to do its work.

Hope's moaning increased as she neared her peak. She held onto Carrie's head as she went over the edge of the wave. Carrie increased the movements from her tongue momentarily and then stilled her mouth but maintained the pressure until she felt Hope begin to relax and the fingers in her hair let loose.

Carrie eased herself up until she was on top of Hope and they were face-to-face. Hope's eyes looked heavy as she opened them to peer at Carrie.

"Well, I checked it out and I think you were right. I think touching my body made you wet. Very wet."

Hope's breathing was beginning to return to normal. "Yeah, that's kind of what I thought was happening. Thanks for checking. Would you like me to check to see if anything similar happens to you?"

Carrie raised her eyes to the ceiling. "Hmm, that might be a good idea. I'll touch you and you can see how my body reacts." She brought her eyes back to Hope's and began to move her fingers down Hope's body again. Hope grabbed her hand, stopping its progress.

"Um, I don't think I can take any more touching at the moment. At least not there."

Carrie trailed her hand back up Hope's body and wrapped her fingers around the firm flesh of one breast. She raked her thumb over the nipple. "How about if I just touch you here then?"

"Yes, I think that will work just fine."

Hope kissed Carrie's mouth, as she moved her fingers down Carrie's body. She weaved her fingers between Carrie's thighs. "It seems that the same thing happens to you, baby," Hope whispered. "The more I check to see how wet you are, the wetter you get." Hope continued until Carrie bucked her hips and a deep moan escaped her mouth.

They stayed wrapped in each other's arms for what seemed like an eternity. But an eternity didn't seem long enough for Carrie.

"Hope?" Carrie asked. "What happened to Maria? Do you know?"

"While I was in class, she went to my dorm room and took anything and everything that belonged to her. She practically lived with me so there was a lot of stuff. No note. No explanation. She eliminated all traces of herself from my life. She stopped coming to any classes we had together. Her roommate told me she transferred to another dorm."

"She didn't ever get in touch with you? She just let you go?" Carrie asked.

"Yes. It ripped my heart out."

"I wouldn't have been able to handle that. If you left this morning and wouldn't talk to me, I think I would go crazy."

"I'm not going anywhere, Carrie." She kissed her lightly on the mouth.

"Have you ever thought about trying to find her?"

"I did try when she first left. But gave up soon after. Her absence and silence made it perfectly clear she was done with me. As much as I wanted to chase after her, I knew it was futile."

"I'm so sorry that happened to you."

"It sounds so stupid now to say I ended up with Tom because a girl broke my heart."

"A broken heart can make us do some crazy things."

"I don't want to think about Maria today. I just want to think about you."

"What a great thing to think about," Carrie said, "Want to make me breakfast while you're thinking?" Carrie grinned at Hope.

"I thought you were the cook in this family."

"Oh, I like that. *Family.*"

"Okay, I guess I can make breakfast. Do you want Cheerios or Rice Krispies?" Hope slipped out of Carrie's arms. "You go take a shower and wash some of my loving off of you and I'll make breakfast." She kissed Carrie on the cheek.

"How come you aren't taking a shower with me?" Carrie whined.

"You just ordered me to make you breakfast."

"What I meant to do was order you to take a shower with me."

"Oh. I guess I misunderstood what you wanted."

Carrie pulled Hope back into her arms. "What I wanted was you. Next to me. All soaped up in the shower. So, I could do more of this..." She kissed Hope softly on the mouth. "I've wanted to do that forever."

"How come you didn't?"

"I thought you would go running."

"And I did. I'm sorry."

"I'm just glad you came back. What about that shower?"

"I'll think about it," Hope said.

Carrie pulled her closer and kissed her with more passion.

"All right. I thought about it. I'll take a shower with you."

Carrie led the way to the bathroom pulling Hope by the hand. It was a long while before they started breakfast.

CHAPTER EIGHTEEN

It had been a week since they had become lovers. Hope had never been happier in her life. They had spent several nights together at one house or the other. This morning they were waking up in Hope's bed.

"Mmm, morning," Carrie said, as she nuzzled into Hope's neck.

Hope wrapped her arms around her. "Morning, honey." Hope savored the feeling of Carrie's naked body pressed against her and Carrie's hand gently stroking her back.

"What would you like to do today? Anything special?" Carrie asked.

"Hmm, well, after you make mad passionate love to me, I think we should read the Sunday paper, and see if there are any good sales. I'm thinking Christmas presents here. Or maybe we can take in a movie if anything looks good."

"I was thinking I would slip out for a little while later today and visit Gram."

"Would you like me to go with you?" Hope asked her.

"I appreciate that, but no. If Gram was herself, up and awake and all, then, yes, I would love for you to meet her. I know she would love you. But I would rather have you know my grandmother from my stories and memories and not by the old lady sleeping in the bed. Does that make sense?"

It did. "That's fine. I just wanted to be there to support you, but I understand." Hope kissed Carrie's nose.

A knock on the bedroom door made them both jump. Another quick knock. The door opened, and Derrick took a step into the room.

"Ma—" he said. The word seemed to stick in his throat.

Hope pulled the sheet up higher around them. "Derrick!" She wasn't sure who was more shocked, her or Derrick.

All the blood seemed to drain from Derrick's face. His eyes went wide and his jaw slack. "Holy shit! Holy fucking shit!" He backed out of the room as suddenly as he had entered.

"Derrick," Hope called after him. "Derrick, go downstairs. I'll be there in a minute." *Holy shit is right. What the hell was he doing home? How am I going to explain this?*

"I'm assuming that was Derrick," Carrie said.

"Yeah, and he's home for vacation a day early. I'm so sorry." Hope felt like all the wind had been knocked out of her. "What am I going to tell him?"

"I know I'm not a mother, but I think you should tell him the truth. I'm going to get dressed and leave the two of you alone." Carrie gathered her clothes from where they had landed in haste the night before and went into the bathroom. Hope put her clothes on and finger combed her hair in record time. She was dressed by the time Carrie emerged.

"At least let me introduce you. I don't want it to look like you are sneaking out. We have nothing to be ashamed of here." Hope hesitated. "I'm just not sure what words to use to explain this."

Carrie gave Hope a quick squeeze. "It will come to you, honey. It'll be fine. Let's go do this." She took Hope's hand and led her out of the room and downstairs. They dropped hands as they approached the bottom steps.

Derrick was sitting on the couch, tapping his foot repeatedly, a nervous habit he had had since he was little. It always came out when he was stressed.

"Derrick this is my friend, Carrie." Hope inwardly cringed at the word friend. The word wasn't nearly accurate enough. "Carrie, this is my son, Derrick."

"Nice to meet you, Derrick." Carrie held out her hand.

"Whatever," Derrick said, ignoring the offered hand.

"Derrick." Hope let her annoyance show. This wasn't the way he was raised. Of course, walking in on your mother and her female lover probably wasn't anything he had ever expected. Hope supposed it was normal for manners to go out the window at a time like this. But still, treating Carrie rudely was unacceptable.

Carrie grabbed her coat from the overstuffed chair where she had tossed it the evening before and slipped it on. Hope was glad that was the only piece of clothing they had left lying around. There were nights when the living room floor was strewn with clothes they discarded in their rush to get to the bedroom.

"Call me later," Carrie said to Hope. Hope nodded. Carrie silently slipped out the front door, closing it behind her.

Hope sat across from Derrick. "I think we need to talk about what's happening here." Hope consciously kept her voice gentle and even, despite her irritation at his rude behavior.

"I think I can figure that one out," Derrick said, not trying to hide his anger.

"Derrick, listen to me, please. Let me explain." She waited for his response, but he only shook his head.

She ignored it and went on. "I met Carrie a few months ago and we became friends. We spent a lot of time together. We had dinners together and went to the movies and she even taught me to bowl. I didn't plan it and I didn't expect it, but I developed feelings for her. Deep feelings."

"How can you have feelings for her Mom? You're not a lesbian."

"Stop it, Derrick. I have a right to be with her. I have a right to be happy."

"But you can't be a lesbian." He turned to look at her. "Because if you're a lesbian, then everything you had with Dad was a lie. Nothing but a lie."

Hope stood. "No. I had *you* with your father and *you* are not a lie. We were a family. But your father's gone. I want to be with Carrie. She makes me happy."

"But you were married to Dad for a long time and now you want to be with a woman? What happened to the rules?"

"What rules? There are no rules in this. There are no rules in love." Hope ran her hand through her hair. "Derrick, I would really like you to understand this and accept it."

"I don't want to accept this. I don't want you to do this. You were in Dad's bed with her. He's been dead less than a year and you were in Dad's bed." He spit the words out at her.

This wasn't going well. Hope felt the anger rising in her. She needed to calm down and explain this the right way. "He was sick for three years. Three years," she said a little louder than she had intended. "It's not his bed, Derrick. It's *my* bed. I have a right to have whoever I want in that bed. I think I put my life on hold long enough. I have a right to live and a right to be with someone."

"I can't take this right now. This is just too much at once. I gotta go." He stood and grabbed his coat from the arm of the couch.

Hope stepped in front of her son to keep him from leaving. "Where are you going?"

He hesitated as if he was deciding whether to answer her or not. Finally, he said, "Starbucks. I'm meeting Erin there in a little while."

"Are you coming back here?" Hope needed more time to calm down and figure out how to explain this better.

"I don't know. I just need time, Mom. You just kind of dumped this all on me at once, ya know, and it sucks. It just sucks." Derrick stepped around her and headed for the door without another word.

Hope stared after him. This wasn't the way she intended to tell Derrick about Carrie. She sank down into the chair and shook her head. She knew she needed to give him time. She reached for the phone and called Carrie.

❖

It was dark by the time Derrick came back. Hope was sitting in a chair in the living room trying to concentrate on the book she was reading when he came in, followed by Erin.

"Hi," Hope said, trying to get a handle on Derrick's mood.

"Hi," Erin said to her. She bumped her shoulder into Derrick.

He glared at her before turning to his mother. "Hi," he said so quietly Hope could barely hear him.

Hope put her book on the end table. "I'm glad you came back. Are you guys hungry? Can I get you something to eat?" She rose out of her chair.

"No, thanks," Erin told her. "We ate a little while ago." She sat on the couch and pulled Derrick's hand until he sat next to her.

Hope sat again. She wasn't sure what to say. Should she try to explain further? Should she ignore the situation and just make small talk? She looked over at her son for a clue. His foot tapped out a nervous rhythm on the floor, his eyes glued to the area rug under his feet.

Erin broke the silence. "I know this is none of my business, but Derrick told me what happened. I really think the two of you need to talk about this. I'm going to go upstairs to leave you alone." She began to get up but Derrick stopped her.

"I want you to stay," he told her. Erin looked over at Hope silently waiting for her opinion.

"It's fine if you stay," Hope said. Erin nodded. Hope looked at Derrick. "I don't want this to be a problem between us, Derrick."

Derrick looked at his mother, his eyes dark. "I am really having a hard time with this, Mom. I came home a day early to surprise you, and I walk in to this crap."

"I was going to tell you. It wasn't my intention for you to find out the way you did."

"I don't want you to replace Dad." His foot tapped faster.

"I know that," Hope said. She kept her voice soft. She could understand his pain and the last thing she wanted to do was add to it. "I'm not trying to replace him. I'm just trying to get on with my life. I didn't plan on this happening, but I'm not willing to give it up because it makes you uncomfortable. Being with Carrie makes me very happy, and I'd like for you to understand and accept that."

"I don't want you to be unhappy, Mom, but damn, it seems so quick to me and it's just so weird and messed up."

"I think you need time to get used to this. All I ask is that you try. Can you do that for me?"

"I'll try," Derrick said. "Do you have any cookies or anything? I could really go for some Oreos."

Hope laughed. It was good to know some things never changed.

CHAPTER NINETEEN

Is your *girlfriend* coming with us to Grandma's for Thanksgiving?" Derrick asked Hope the next morning over his bowl of Cheerios.

Hope looked at him, trying to decide if he was trying to make an effort at accepting the situation or if he was being sarcastic. Still not sure, she answered him. "No, she's spending it with her mother, and they are going to visit her grandmother in the nursing home."

"So, who's gonna be there?" He brought the bowl to his mouth to drink the last drops of milk. It was a habit Hope hated but tolerated. It was one of those things in life that wasn't worth fighting over.

"Let's see. I'll be there..."

"Very funny," he said.

"And you and Erin, Grandma, Grandpa, Aunt Marcy, Uncle Bert, and the kids." She paused. "I would appreciate if you didn't mention Carrie to anyone at Thanksgiving."

"Are you ashamed of her? Is she your dirty little secret?" Derrick asked. Yep. He was being sarcastic.

She set her coffee cup down and gave him her full attention. "No, I am not ashamed of her, and I don't appreciate you talking like this. I haven't told anybody about Carrie yet and them finding out from you is not the way I want to do it." She looked intently at him, waiting for his response.

"Okay, okay," he said, getting up. "I won't say anything." He started out of the room.

Hope cleared her throat loudly, causing Derrick to turn back around. She motioned to his bowl and spoon still on the table. Without another word, he picked them up, put them in the dishwasher, and left the room.

Erin came down the stairs as Hope was getting ready to leave for work. "Help yourself to anything you want to eat in the kitchen. There should be cereal if Derrick didn't eat it all."

"Thanks," Erin said, trying to rub the sleep from her eyes. "Where is he?"

"I am pretty sure he went into the family room to play video games. I have to get going to work. Make yourself at home and I'll see you later." Hope took her keys from the hook hanging by the door and left.

As soon as she was in her car, Hope called Carrie.

"Hi, sweetie," Carrie answered. "How are things this morning?"

"Hi. If you're talking about Derrick, his attitude is slightly better than yesterday, but he still has a ways to go."

"It's going to take time. This is all very new to him. Am I going to see you tonight?" Carrie asked.

"I wish I could say yes, but I'm afraid not. My sister invited us over for dinner. But do you have any plans tomorrow after work? Are you visiting your grandmother tomorrow?"

"I'm going after work today. What did you have in mind?"

Hope headed in the direction of work. If felt good to be talking to Carrie, but she wished she could see her beautiful face and feel her arms around her.

"I don't care as long as I get to see you. We could go out for Chinese."

"That sounds great. Do you want to invite Derrick and Erin?" Carrie asked.

"No, I want to be alone with you. They have plans with friends anyway ." Hope paused. "I think it might be a little soon for him. I do want the two of you to get to know each other, but I think I would like to wait just a little longer. Is that all right?" Anxiety settled in her stomach as she waited for Carrie to answer.

"I can understand that. It's fine."

"I'll be over around six tomorrow if that works for you."

"Okay, honey. I'll see you then."

"Call me when you get home tonight."

"You got it. Bye."

Hope hung up. How was she going to get Derrick to understand and accept her relationship with Carrie?

CHAPTER TWENTY

Carrie rushed to the door as soon as she heard Hope's car in the driveway. She flung the door open, grabbed Hope by the collar of her coat, and yanked her in. She closed the door and smothered Hope with kisses.

"Oh my," Hope said when Carrie let her up for air.

"I missed you."

"I guess you did. I like it when you miss me." Hope pulled her in for a few more kisses.

"Do you want to go out for Chinese?" Carrie asked. "Or we could stay here and order in. Or we could stay here and not eat *food*, at all."

"Hmmm, let's order in and cuddle up on the couch until it gets here. How about that?"

"I'm thinking that's a good plan." She pulled Hope over to the couch and down until Hope was lying on top of her. "How's this for cuddling?"

"Mmm. This works."

Carrie's body reacted immediately to Hope being so close. Sometimes it still amazed her. She ran her fingers through Hope's hair and pulled her face down until their lips were touching. Carrie ran her tongue around the inside edge of Hope's lips before exploring the inside. Her heart rate picked up speed as the wetness in her center increased.

"How are we going to order Chinese food from this position?" Hope asked when she regained momentary control of her own mouth.

"Oh, yeah, Chinese food. We were going to order Chinese food. I'm not as hungry as I was before. I am not sure I need food anymore," Carrie said. "I think I just need you."

"Well, my little love bug, I'm starving. I haven't eaten anything since breakfast, and if I don't eat something I am going to pass out from hunger."

"Will anything do or do you have to eat Chinese food?" Carrie wiggled her eyebrows.

"I'm thinking I should start with Chinese food and then maybe later on I can eat what you have in mind." Hope blushed.

"What if I was thinking about eating homemade chocolate chip cookies?" Carrie kissed Hope lightly on the lips.

"I guess that would be a different story. We could have Chinese food, cookies, and then—" Hope didn't finish. Her words where cut off by Carrie's deep kiss.

Carrie eased Hope up and off of her until they were both sitting. She handed Hope her cell phone. "Go ahead and call in the order for delivery. Maybe we'll eat the cookies while we're waiting for it. That way we can get done eating faster and get to the good stuff." She planted tiny kisses on Hope's neck and chest as Hope pushed the speed dial number for the Chinese restaurant Carrie had programmed into the phone.

"Yes," she said when someone answered. She cleared her throat, but it still sounded a little rough around the edges. Carrie enjoyed the flustered tone to Hope's voice as she continued with the kisses. She pushed Hope's shirt up around her neck and her hands kneaded Hope's breasts. "I would like to place an order for delivery. Yes, I would like—um—the—um—the beef and broccoli, the moo goo gai pan, pork lo mein and two egg rolls. Umm, the name is Hope. Seventeen West Melborn Street. Yes, thank you." She hit the end button on the phone. "About twenty minutes," she said to Carrie with the little bit of breath she seemed to have left.

"Twenty minutes? What are we going to do with twenty whole minutes?" She continued moving her hands over Hope's breasts. She pushed Hope's bra up and stroked bare skin. Hope's nipples hardened under her touch.

"What can we possibly do in twenty minutes?" Hope whispered.

"We could do this." Carrie squeezed the firm flesh of Hope's breast.

Hope closed her eyes and let out a deep sigh. The sound hit Carrie directly in her center.

"Or we could do this." Carrie took a firm nipple between her thumb and finger and gently rolled it. She moved her hand down the length of Hope's body to the waistband of her pants. "Or we could do—"

Hope grabbed her hand. "That, we can't do, because I wouldn't want you to stop, and we are going to need to answer the door pretty soon. I want more than twenty minutes for that."

"What if I moved my hand really fast?" Carrie asked.

"What if I did this instead?" Hope put her lips on Carrie's neck and began to alternate kisses with sucking and licking Carrie's skin. Carrie closed her eyes and took a deep breath. Her whole body relaxed under the magic of Hope's mouth.

They were still kissing when the doorbell rang. Carrie reluctantly slid off of the couch, straightened her bra and shirt, and answered the door. Hope went to the kitchen to round up plates and drinks.

"Just so you know..." Carrie set the food on the coffee table. "I want to throw you on the floor and make love to you right now." Just saying the words sent a surge through her. She smiled. "But don't worry. I am going to let you eat first. I might even let you have a cookie. But then I am going to have my way with you."

Hope smiled. "Okay," was her simple answer.

Carrie made herself comfortable on the floor in front of the coffee table, took the plate Hope offered her, and grabbed a set of chopsticks from the bag. She wasn't about to admit it, but she was hungry and glad they decided to get food delivered. She wasted no time eating and finished before Hope did.

"Are you just going to sit there and watch me eat?" Hope asked her.

"Yes. The minute you get done I am going to pounce on you. You got a problem with that?" Carrie gave her most seductive smile.

Hope set her plate on the coffee table, stood, and put her hand out to Carrie. "Come on," she said.

"You haven't finished eating."

"You're more important than the food."

"It doesn't have to be a choice. I'll wait."

"I can't wait any more. So, come on." Carrie took her hand and allowed Hope to pull her to her feet and lead her to the bedroom.

CHAPTER TWENTY-ONE

"M om. We're ready to go," Derrick called up the stairs. Hope buttoned the last two buttons on her blouse. It was one of her favorites. She loved the deep burgundy color and silky feel. A quick look in the mirror while she tucked the shirttail into her cream-colored slacks and she was almost ready. "I'll be down in a few minutes," she yelled. *Where's my belt?* She found it in the back of the closet.

The TV was blaring the Macy's Thanksgiving Day Parade, but Derrick and Erin didn't seem to be watching it. They were far more interested in making out, as they snuggled together on the couch.

"Turn that off and we'll get going," Hope said.

"Finally," Derrick replied. Apparently, he was still irritated with her.

Erin swatted him in the chest with the back of her hand. Hope was grateful for her intervention. She really did like this girl.

"You look very nice," Erin said to Hope. Erin was dressed in a neat yellow blouse tucked into brown dress pants. Hope was glad Derrick at least had on clean jeans and a decent button-down shirt, instead of an old T-shirt that was his usual attire.

"Thank you very much, Erin. You do too." Hope smiled at her. "Would you go get the pie I bought, Derrick? It's on the counter by the stove in the kitchen." She grabbed their coats while Derrick retrieved the dessert.

Twenty minutes later, Hope pulled up in front of her parents' house. She felt like she was missing something and realized it was Carrie. She knew at some point soon she would have to tell her family about Carrie. She *wanted* to tell them. She just wasn't sure *when* or just what she was going to say.

Derrick and Erin were halfway up the walk by the time Hope got out of the car. She sped up to catch them before they reached the front door. Derrick rang the doorbell, balancing the pie on his palm.

His grandfather opened the door. "Hi, Grandpa."

"Derrick!" Hope's dad said, "I swear you get taller every time I see you." He patted Derrick on the back. "Hello, welcome," he said to Erin.

"Hi, Dad. How are you?" Hope gave her father a hug. She noticed a little more gray hair around his temples, but he was still a handsome man. "This is Erin, Derrick's girlfriend."

"Very nice to meet you," Erin said.

"You too. Well, come on in. Derrick, hand me that pie and why don't you take all your coats and put them on the bed in the spare bedroom at the end of the hall."

"Your mother's in the kitchen," he said to Hope. "Follow me and I'll get you something to drink." Derrick disappeared down the hallway.

"Hi, Mom," Hope said as they entered the kitchen. Her mother turned around, turkey baster in her hand.

"Hello, honey." Her mother looked her up and down. "Your hair's a little too long don't you think? I like it much better shorter." She put the baster on the counter and smoothed her apron. She had a different one for each occasion. This one sported a turkey wearing a pilgrim hat. It protected a stylish turquoise pantsuit. As usual, every silver hair on her head was in its proper place and tightly held there with a generous layer of hairspray. Her cheeks were rosy red from a combination of heat in the kitchen and a fair amount of blush. "Hello," she said looking at Erin.

"Mom, this is Erin, Derrick's girlfriend. Erin, my mother, Mrs. Carver," Hope said, ignoring the comment about her hair.

Erin stepped forward with her hand out. "Hello." Hope's mother shook the hand that was offered to her. "It's nice to meet you."

"She's cute," she said to Hope, as if Erin wasn't there.

"Thanks," Derrick said as he joined them in the kitchen. "She *is* pretty darn cute." He put his arm around Erin. "Hi, Grandma."

His grandmother stretched her arms out. "Come and give me a hug, Derrick." He was much taller than her and had to reach down to embrace her.

"What would you like to drink?" Hope's dad asked them. "We have root beer, ginger ale, and Pepsi. We also have wine, but you kids are too young for that."

"I'll take a beer." Derrick smiled.

"You are such a wise guy, just like your mother," Hope's dad responded. "You'll take soda pop, or water, young man."

"Pepsi, Grandpa," he said.

"And you, young lady?" he asked Erin.

"The same please."

He winked at Hope. "Polite. I like that." He poured and distributed the drinks, giving Hope a glass of wine. "I know you'll need this," he whispered.

As usual, Hope's mother insisted she didn't need any help and the guests were shuttled out of the kitchen and into the living room. Several minutes later, Marcy arrived with her family in tow. The twins made a beeline for their cousin Derrick, while Marcy and her husband disappeared in the kitchen. Derrick scooped both kids up in his arms and had them giggling before long as he gently tossed them around.

Marcy called them her miracle babies. After years of trying unsuccessfully to get pregnant, she and her husband had finally turned to doctors and fertility drugs. The two seven-year-old boys were the happy results.

"Hey," Derrick told them. "If you guys don't go say hi to Grandma in the kitchen, she is gonna beat your butts."

"Okay," they giggled in unison.

"Come back when you're done," he called after them.

It didn't take long for Marcy and her husband to get kicked out of the kitchen and settle down with the rest of the family in the living room. Everyone was on their best behavior and Hope enjoyed the small talk. She kept one eye on Derrick. He seemed to be enjoying himself too despite Hope's worry about him missing his father. The fact that Erin was with him helped, Hope was sure. She breathed a sigh of relief.

Throughout the course of the day, Hope's thoughts kept returning to Carrie. She missed her, plain and simple. After her last bite of dessert, she excused herself and went into the spare bedroom and called her. She felt an undeniable rush when Carrie answered the phone and Hope heard her voice.

"I miss you," Hope started the conversation. "I'm not calling at a bad time, am I?"

"There is never a bad time to talk to you. What are you doing?" Carrie asked.

"At the moment I'm sitting on a bed full of coats."

"Is that a family tradition?"

"Yes, as a matter of fact it is. Every Thanksgiving, one person in our family gets to sit in here with the coats. This year I'm the lucky one. What are you doing?"

"Nothing nearly as exciting," Carrie said. Hope could hear her smile through the phone line. "My Mom made a turkey breast in the good old Nesco roaster. We finished eating a little while ago."

"Where's your mom now?"

"She's putting the leftovers away. I was banished to the living room. She likes to clean up alone."

"That's how my mom likes to cook, but she makes us all help her clean. I think they are all cleaning up now."

"So that means you're not helping?"

"I have something much more important to do."

"And what would that be?"

"I have to hear my girlfriend's voice,"

"You've never called me that before. Your girlfriend."

Hope lowered her voice even though she was away from the rest of her family. "Well, it's either that or my lesbian lover. Which do you prefer?"

"Hmm, I like being both. And I miss you too."

A knock on the door made Hope jump. Derrick stuck his head in the room. "Grandma's starting to wonder where you are. I didn't know what to say so I told her you were looking for something in your coat."

Hope moved the phone away from her mouth. "Thanks, Derrick. I'll be out in a minute."

He nodded and pulled the door closed. A moment later, he opened it again and whispered. "Tell Carrie I said hi." His smile seemed genuine. He closed the door again.

"I have to go, honey—and Derrick said to tell you hi." Hope didn't try to hide her surprise. "I wonder if Erin talked to him?"

"He did? I guess that is a good sign. Okay, sweetie. Call me tonight. Have fun with your family."

"Bye, Carrie," Hope said. She held the phone to her chest for several seconds after she hung up.

CHAPTER TWENTY-TWO

Hope put her key in the door and was about to turn it when she realized the door was already unlocked. She searched her mind to remember if she had locked it on the way out. She was certain she had. Carrie was due to come over, but it was much too early for her to be here, and besides, the key she had made for her was still sitting on her desk. She hadn't given it to her yet. Derrick had returned to school three days ago after Thanksgiving break and wasn't due back home until December eighteenth. There was no car in the driveway.

She turned the knob and slowly pushed the door open. *This might not be a good idea. What if someone broke in and is still in the house?*

She stuck just her head in the open door, prepared to run if necessary. "Hello?" she called out softly. "Hello?" she repeated a little louder.

"Hi, Mom." Derrick stepped into the room from the kitchen. Startled, Hope dropped her keys on the hardwood floor.

"You scared the shit out of me." She stooped to pick up the keys and continued into the house.

"Language, Mom." Derrick laughed, but Hope sensed an underlying tension. Something wasn't right.

"Never mind my language. What are you doing here? And where's your car?" Hope deposited her keys on the end table and her coat on the couch. She waited for Derrick to answer. "Is everything all right?"

"Erin has my car. She dropped me off—and *I* think everything's all right. I'm not sure you are going to think that." Derrick swallowed hard and avoided looking her in the eye.

"What is that supposed to mean?" Hope asked, not trying to hide her concern.

"I think I need a glass of water." Derrick disappeared into the kitchen. Hope followed closely behind.

Derrick filled a glass with filtered water from the fridge and drank half of it. "Mom, you might want to sit down."

She put her hands on her hips, her concern was overshadowed by her growing impatience. "Just tell me what's going on."

"I'm getting married, Mom." The words spilled out of Derrick's mouth almost faster than Hope could comprehend them.

"You're what? Who are you marrying? Are you marrying Erin?" Hope asked, confused. *Why? Why now? He's far too young and still in school. What the hell?*

"Of course I'm marrying Erin. Who else would you think I'd marry?" Derrick's annoyance was evident.

"All right, let's back up here. Are you telling me you're engaged to Erin and you are getting married *after* you both graduate from college?" *Please. Please say you are waiting until you're out of school.*

"No, Mom. I mean we are getting married now. Like in the near future."

"No, I don't think so." She tried to control her voice, but the volume rose considerably. "That would just be stupid."

"Please, Mom, just hear me out." Derrick kept his voice calm and even, only adding to Hope's confusion. "Erin—we—Erin and I are going to have a baby. Erin's pregnant."

A wave of nauseating heat rushed through Hope. She closed her eyes against her rising panic. She opened them to find Derrick watching her, waiting for her response. "Oh, Derrick. No. You didn't."

Hope wasn't naive enough to think her son wouldn't have sex before marriage, but she had begun talking to him about the importance of birth control when he was only thirteen. She was careful not to lecture him, but to educate him so he would never be in the same position she found herself in when she was a teenager. She made sure he had access to condoms. She made sure she or his father were always available for questions. She made sure. *I guess I didn't make sure enough. He got his girlfriend pregnant anyway. Oh my God.*

"It's all right, Mom. Honest it is. This will all work out."

"Derrick, how could…" She didn't finish the question. She knew how this thing could happen. She didn't need to ask.

"Why do you have to get married? You are both so young."

"We want to get married. We want to be together. You don't want us to get married?"

"Just for the record, I am a huge fan of living in sin," Hope said.

"Since when?" Derrick asked. "I thought I raised you better than that, Mom." Derrick said, obviously trying to be funny.

Hope wasn't seeing the humor in it. "Since my nineteen-year-old son announced he is getting married. Derrick, you are way too young." She knew she was repeating herself.

"I'm just about the same age you were when you got married."

"Then you know that I know what I'm talking about." Hope wasn't sure she was making sense. All she saw when she looked at him was her little boy throwing his life away. The same way she had. She also saw the determination in his eyes.

"You aren't going to change my mind, Mom. I love Erin. I really love her. I thought if anyone would understand that it would be you. Aren't you the one who told me there are no rules in love?" He used air quotes and flashed a smile at her.

"No fair, Derrick, using my own words against me." Hope felt like she was losing this round.

"Mom, I just want you to be happy for me. I know it won't be easy. I am willing to do whatever I have to do to make sure Erin and the baby have whatever they need. I am going to make this work. We love each other."

"And what about Erin? How does she feel about all this? Does she want to get married?" Hope couldn't help but think about herself in the same situation at a young age. She hadn't wanted to get married, but she did it anyway. She did what she thought everyone expected her to do, what was right for her baby. Her baby was standing here now telling her he was going to make the same mistake she had. It was breaking her heart.

"I told Erin I would stand by her whatever she wanted to do. She told me she loves me, Mom. She wants to get married and raise the baby together. I know we can do it." Derrick sat at the table and leaned the chair back on two legs. "Sit down, Mom. Let's talk about this like two adults."

"Adults don't sit in chairs like that."

Derrick smiled. Hope had to give him credit for keeping his cool. "Just can't help but think of me as your little boy, can you?"

"You *are* my little boy. I know you are growing up and want to make your own decisions, but you are too young to get married." Hope began to raise her voice, again.

"Mom, you need to calm down and let me explain."

"Don't tell me to calm down. There is no being calm about this." Hope knew calming down was exactly what she should be doing, but the thought just made her more upset. "This is not how I wanted your life to go. This isn't what we planned for you."

Derrick's tone changed to defensive mode. "You don't get to plan my life for me. I'm old enough to make my own decisions. I've decided to marry Erin and that's what I'm going to do. I was really hoping you would support us on this. But you aren't going to change my mind."

Hope found it difficult to breathe. *Please, dear God, don't let my son go through what I did. Don't let him make the same mistakes. Please let me find the right words to say to him to make him understand.*

Hope closed her eyes and rubbed her temples in an attempt to compose herself. She took a deep breath, opened her eyes, and looked directly at Derrick. "You are making the biggest mistake of your life."

Derrick's face turned a deep shade of red. "It's my life and I am going to live it the way I want to." He raised his voice to her, something he hadn't done since he was six years old. "I *am* going to marry Erin and we *are* going to have this baby. There isn't anything you are going to say that is going to change my mind." He stormed out of the kitchen and out the front door. It slammed behind him.

Hope stared after him. Her world imploded in the blink of an eye. Her son was about to ruin his life and there was nothing she could do about it. Nothing.

CHAPTER TWENTY-THREE

Carrie knocked again and wondered why Hope wasn't answering the door. Her car was in the driveway. Carrie started to get worried. She pulled her cell phone from her pocket to call Hope when the door opened.

"Hi," Carrie said as she entered the house. Hope had obviously been crying. "What's wrong?" Carrie pulled her into a hug. "Honey?"

"My son. My son is what's wrong." Hope sat heavily on the couch.

"What's wrong with Derrick?" Carrie asked, sitting next to her. "Is he okay?"

"That depends on what you mean by okay. He is about to throw his life away. He won't listen to me at all."

Carrie could clearly see Hope was very upset, but still wasn't sure what the problem was. When Hope didn't continue on her own, Carrie asked, "What's he doing?"

"He's getting married." Hope reached for the box of tissues on the arm of the couch and wiped her nose.

"Oh, my God, is that all? You had me scared it was something really bad." Carrie patted Hope's knee.

Hope stared at her. "This *is* really bad. My son is about to throw his life away because he got some girl pregnant." She shook her head.

"Who did he get pregnant?" Carrie asked, not sure what else to say.

"Erin," she said in a sharp tone Carrie had never heard her use before. "Who do you think it would be?"

"Well, the way you said... Never mind. Okay, so Erin is pregnant, and they plan on getting married?"

"Yes. He is much too young to get married. He is making a big mistake. I should know, it's exactly what I did."

"I know you went through a lot of stuff, honey and you're worried about him, but maybe it isn't the same for him." Carrie put her arm around Hope, but Hope shook it off.

"What do you know about it?" Her voice was unusually high-pitched and a little scary. "This changes everything. You don't understand at all."

Carrie's was confused. Hope's reaction seemed much stronger than was warranted. She was speechless for several seconds. "Hope," she said when she found her voice again, "let's calm down here and talk about this."

"Will everyone just stop telling me to calm down. I will not calm down. I really don't want to talk about this right now. I think you should go." Hope stood.

Carrie looked up at Hope, her mouth agape in surprise. "What? We don't have to talk about it if you don't want to, but I wanted to spend the evening with you. I don't want to go."

Without meeting her eyes, Hope said, "I need to be alone. Please go. I'll call you later." When Carrie made no move toward leaving, Hope turned to her. "Please, Carrie."

Without a word, Carrie got up and walked to the door. She opened it and turned back to Hope. She opened her mouth, but no words came out. She wasn't sure how to handle this. She left without saying anything else and closed the door behind her.

CHAPTER TWENTY-FOUR

Carrie didn't hear from Hope at all the rest of that day. She picked up the phone several times but hung it up without dialing. She would just give Hope time to calm down and wait for her to call.

She got very little sleep that night, tossing and turning with bits and pieces of bad dreams wafting in and out of her mind. She finally fell into a sound sleep at five o'clock in the morning. A sleep that was shattered by the sound of her cell phone ringing.

Carrie looked at the clock. Six thirty. Who would be calling her at six thirty in the morning? *Hope? It must be Hope.* She picked up her phone from the nightstand and blinked to try to force her eyes into focus. She pressed the talk button on the phone and put it to her ear.

"Carrie?" It was her mother. Carrie was instantly awake.

"Mom. Mom what is it? Is it Gram? Did something happen to Gram?" She sat up in bed, her whole being on high alert

"The nursing home just called me. She has pneumonia. It isn't good when a person in a coma has pneumonia." She could hear the tears in her mother's voice.

"What can we do, Mom? What are we supposed to do?"

"There's nothing we can do. They moved her from the nursing home back to the hospital. They are trying to keep her comfortable and get it under control. I just thought you should know. I'm going to call your brothers as soon as I hang up from you."

"Okay, Mom, thanks for letting me know. I'm going to get dressed and go see her before I go to work. I'll talk to you later."

"Yes. I thought you would want to see her. She's on the fourth floor. Call me when you get a break at work later. Bye, honey."

"Bye, Mom." Carrie pushed back the covers, not caring that some of the blanket ended up in a heap on the floor. She went through her morning routine as quickly as she could, changing out of her pajamas and into her work clothes and headed out the door.

It took only twenty minutes to get to the hospital and up to the fourth floor. Those twenty minutes seemed like an eternity to Carrie. A quick stop at the nurses' station told her which room her grandmother was in. She could tell immediately there was a change in her. The sound of Gram's breathing was labored and an IV hung by her bed with a tube attached to her arm.

The main light in the room was turned off, and only a small light attached to the wall above the headboard shed light in the dimly lit room. Carrie walked to the windows and pulled open the cord on the blinds to let in some of the morning light.

Sitting on the side of the bed, Carrie picked up her grandmother's hand and held it tight, willing her grandmother to open her eyes. And knowing she wouldn't. Carrie smoothed down her hair. She looked so frail and helpless lying in a bed that seemed much too big for her. Even more so than she seemed in the nursing home. This was not the woman she knew. Not the woman she had grown up with.

She sat for a long time just watching her grandmother breathe. One harsh breath in, one harsh breath out.

Carrie pulled the covers back and gently slipped in next to her grandmother, careful not to disturb the IV line, and wrapped her arms around her. "Grammie," she said softly. "I want you to wake up and talk to me. I want you to wake up and tell me a story about when you were a little girl and you used to skinny dip in the river, or about the time your brother Albert put a frog down your back. I miss you, Gram." Carrie let sad, angry tears slide down her cheeks. They were cool on her hot skin. "But I know that's not going to happen. So, I want you to be able to leave here. I want to tell you it's okay to leave us now. I'll take care of Mom. I promise. It can't be much fun for you just hanging out like this. It's time to go join your parents and Grandpa. I know you've missed him an awful lot since he died. I'm sure he's missed you, too. I know he's waiting for you, Gram."

Carrie paused to let a small sob escape. The tears filling Carrie's eyes made her grandmother look bleary, as if in a dream. "It's time to stop fighting this. I love you and I will miss you, always. I couldn't have asked for a better grandma or a better friend. But I want you to be happy and free again, and you can't do that here. So, please, Gram. Please go." Carrie continued to cry softly. The tears fell on the pillow and on her grandmother's shoulder. She remained in that position for a long while, just holding onto the little bit of life that was still her beloved grandmother.

❖

Carrie had a lot of trouble keeping her mind on work. She arrived late but didn't really care. Not today. Her mind vacillated between her grandmother taking a turn for the worse and the argument with Hope the day before. She still wasn't sure what had happened there, and why Hope had gotten so upset with her.

She wanted so badly to call Hope and tell her about Gram, but she didn't. She would just give Hope some time. *She'll call me when she's ready. But please, Hope, please don't take too long.*

Feeling like she was sleepwalking through her day, Carrie paid no attention at the managers meeting before lunch and only briefly spoke to Jeff, the head of security during her cursory tour of the warehouse. The rest of the day was spent in her office doing absolutely nothing. As much as she tried to work, she found herself just staring at her computer screen until the screen saver kicked in. She made two phone calls, one to her mother and one to the hospital to check on her grandmother. There was no change. Carrie felt helpless and restless. And alone.

❖

Hope did her best to keep a smile on her face while she made small talk with her co-workers and patients. Her thoughts wandered constantly and she fought to bring them back to the task at hand. She needed to pay attention as she scraped the tartar from a patient's teeth. She wasn't sure she would make it through the day.

There had to be some way to convince Derrick he was making a mistake. She had gotten married far too young and now she felt her son was doing the same thing. And she had yelled at Carrie about it. Carrie didn't deserve that. She took her anger and fear out on Carrie. She needed to make it right. With great difficulty, she pushed the thought of Carrie momentarily away, so she could work. But as soon as Carrie was pushed to the back of her mind, Derrick would enter stage left.

Hope wanted what was best for her son and Erin too, for that matter. Getting married would force them into a situation they didn't want—into a life they didn't want. It would stop them from pursuing the lives they deserved and limit their choices. Just like it had limited hers. She had spent nineteen years in a life that stifled her, that held her back and stopped her from being who she was.

Hope stopped scraping and stared into space. The patient, mouth opened wide, looked at her. It took another moment for Hope to realize she had a person sitting in front of her waiting for her teeth to be cleaned. "Sorry," Hope said and went back to work.

Oh my God. I'm projecting all of my own feelings onto Derrick and Erin. They are going to have a baby and they love each other. They are trying to do the right thing. Instead of supporting my son, I'm pushing him away. I can't protect him by rejecting him. The sudden revelation hit Hope like a rock to the head.

"Rinse and spit, Mrs. Peters," Hope told the patient. "You're all set with your cleaning. Dr. Jenson will be here in a few minutes."

The patient nodded. Hope left the room and stuck her head into the office down the hall.

"Mrs. Peters is ready for her exam in room two," she told her boss. He waved his hand in the air. Hope knew that meant he would meet her in the exam room in a few minutes.

Hope stepped into the break room and sat at the table facing the open door, so she could see when Dr. Jenson passed by on his way to the patient. She pulled her cell phone from her pocket and hit Carrie's number.

Carrie answered immediately. "Hello."

"I am such an ass," Hope said as soon as she heard Carrie's voice. "I am so sorry." There was silence for several moments. "Carrie?" Hope said. She heard a sound and knew Carrie was crying. "Carrie?" she repeated. "Please talk to me."

"My grandmother has pneumonia," Carrie told her. "She isn't doing good."

"Oh, honey, I'm so sorry. I'm so sorry I wasn't there for you. What can I do?" Guilt washed over her.

"There isn't anything anyone can do. I was with her this morning and I'm going to go back after work and meet my mother there."

"Do you want me to go to the nursing home with you?"

"They moved her back to the hospital. There really isn't anything you can do there. But..." Carrie hesitated.

"What? Just tell me. I'll do anything for you."

"Can you come over to my house tonight? I just want to be with you."

Hope saw the doctor walk by the room on the way to examine Mrs. Peter's teeth. "Of course I'll come over. I'll be there by the time you get home from visiting your grandmother. I'll stop and pick up subs. All right?"

"Thank you."

"Of course. I need to get back to work, but I'll see you later. Call and leave a message if you need me."

"I'll see you later. Bye."

"Bye." Hope slipped the phone back into her pocket and headed to room two. She had a lot of making up to do to Carrie. She was going to make sure Carrie knew how sorry she was.

❖

Hope let herself into Carrie's house using the garage door code Carrie had given her the week before. She set the subs on the kitchen table and went into the living room to wait.

Hope knew there was one more phone call she needed to make. She had purposely waited until she had time to compose herself and be sure of what she wanted to say before calling Derrick. She held her phone for several seconds before hitting his number in her contact list.

The phone rang several times before going to voice mail. Hope cleared her throat. "Hi, Derrick, it's Mom. I wanted to say I'm sorry for reacting so strongly yesterday and I would like to be able to talk to you and Erin about this. Calmly. Please give me a call back so we can figure out when we can get together to talk." She paused before adding. "I love you, Derrick."

Hope threw her phone in her purse and dug through it looking for a pen and her small notebook. She found a blank page and worked on a poem while she waited for Carrie. Hope found writing to be soothing, somehow healing, and she was so happy she'd started doing it again. She suspected Carrie's influence had something to do with that. She had written one poem and had an outline for a short story done when she heard Carrie pull into the driveway.

Hope went to meet her at the door and pulled her into a tight hug. "I am so sorry," she whispered. Hope gave Carrie a kiss on the cheek and helped her off with her coat.

"How's your grandmother? Any change?"

They made their way to the kitchen. "She isn't doing well at all." She paused. "This morning I told her she should stop fighting this and go." Tears streamed down her face. "I told her it was okay to die."

Hope swept Carrie into her arms, held her, and stroked her hair. "It's all right, baby. It's all right. You did the right thing."

Carrie sobbed into Hope's shoulder for a few minutes before composing herself.

She swiped at the tears on her cheek. "Thank you for being here. I'm going to the bathroom and clean up a little. I need to wash my face."

"Of course, honey. Do whatever you need to do. I'll get us something to eat." Hope got two plates from the cupboard, unwrapped the subs, and put a half onto each plate, along with a handful of potato chips from the bag she found on the counter. "Do you want a glass of wine?" she asked when Carrie returned.

"No, I am going to skip the alcohol just in case they call from the hospital. I want to be able to drive. Water is fine. She followed Hope into the living room.

Carrie filled Hope in a little more on her grandmother's condition and Hope told Carrie about her more recent thoughts on Derrick and his situation. She apologized again for snapping at Carrie. "It brought me back to my own situation when I was about his age. I felt so helpless and scared then. I projected those same feelings onto his situation. And I was so angry that he let this happen. I guess I wanted you to be as mad at him as I was. When you weren't, I overreacted. I never meant to hurt you." It had taken Hope much of the day to figure out why she had taken her frustration out on Carrie. She would be forever sorry she had.

"You haven't eaten much," Hope said sometime later. She had finished her sub and even polished off a couple of Carrie's homemade cookies.

"I guess I'm not very hungry. Sorry."

Hope could understand that. "No worries. Do you want to get ready for bed? I'll clean up here." Hope gathered the plates.

"Yes, bed sounds like a very good idea."

"Go ahead. I'll be there in a few minutes."

Carrie did as she was told and was already in bed by the time Hope joined her. She pulled Carrie in close and wrapped her arms around her. Carrie kissed her softly on the cheek. "Thank you for being here."

"Of course, sweetie." Hope held onto her as if she would never let her go.

CHAPTER TWENTY-FIVE

Carrie woke as the sun started to peek through the blinds. The clock on the nightstand told her it was six forty-eight. She gingerly extracted herself from Hope's arms and slipped out of bed. After a quick shower, she pulled her wet hair into a ponytail, got dressed, and set the alarm clock on the nightstand for eight a.m. She sat on the edge of the bed and gently shook Hope's shoulder. "Hope," she said quietly.

"Huh?" Hope's voice was groggy and barely audible.

"I'm going to go visit my grandmother. I set the alarm for you so you can get up to go to work. Okay?"

Hope pulled Carrie into an embrace. "You should have woken me." She cleared her throat. It did little to dislodge the sound of sleep. "I would have gotten up with you."

"You were sleeping so peacefully. I didn't want to wake you." Carrie gave her a kiss. "You go back to sleep for a little while. I'll call you later."

Sleep was winning out again as Hope released Carrie. "Okay," she whispered. "I'll talk to you later."

"Bye, baby," Carrie whispered back. She left the room grabbed her coat and headed to the hospital. After yesterday's visit, she wasn't sure what she would find today.

❖

Carrie called work from her grandmother's hospital room to tell them she was taking a personal day and wouldn't be in. Her mother arrived as she was hanging up. Carrie was actually glad to see her. This was too hard to do alone.

"How is she doing?" her mother asked. She rubbed Carrie's shoulder.

"She seems to be getting worse." Carrie patted her mother's hand. "I think it's just a matter of time, Mom."

Her mother nodded. She pulled another chair closer to the bed next to Carrie. Tears streamed down her cheeks and she grabbed the box of Kleenex from the small table by the bed. "I know," her mom said. "I was really hoping she would pull out of this and be her old self. Now I'm not so sure."

"Are Todd and Sammy coming?" She pulled a tissue from the box in her mother's lap and wiped her eyes.

"Sammy should be here tonight. He and Terry and the kids are driving. They're leaving this morning. It's a long drive for them. Todd said he isn't going to be able to come. They are in the middle of some maneuvers or something and the flight itself would be almost fifteen hours with layovers."

"I get that. Gram would understand." She stroked the soft skin on her grandmother's hand, knowing that there wouldn't be too many more opportunities to do that. To touch her. To be with her. She knew the more time that went by the less chance of her grandmother ever waking up. But this. This was almost too much to take. Even though she lost her grandmother when the coma started, as long as she was still breathing, Carrie had held out a little piece of hope, tucked safely away in the back of her heart. Watching her grandmother like this, struggling for every breath, that hope was quickly fading away. Leaving nothing but a hole in Carrie's heart.

They sat without much talking while a parade of doctors, nurses, and medical students made their rounds in and out of the room. There wasn't much to say. Nothing was going to make this better. Nothing.

Later that day, as Carrie held her hand, Gram took her last ragged breath and left the confines of her broken body to be free in the expanse of the universe.

"No more suffering, Gram," Carrie said through a cascade of tears. "Tell Grandpa I said hi and I love him. I love you, too, Gram. I always will."

❖

"Oh, Carrie, I'm so sorry." Hope gathered Carrie in her arms. She knew as soon as she opened her door and took one look at Carrie's face that it wasn't good. "I know how much you loved her." She led Carrie to the couch. "How is your mom doing?"

"I think she's in shock. She was in denial for so long. I know this is hard on her." Carrie had cried so much at the hospital she didn't think she had any tears left. She realized she was wrong as more tears rolled down her cheeks. She brushed them away. "I need to get myself together. I have to meet my mother at the funeral home to make arrangements soon, and my brother Sammy should be here tonight with his family. They're driving in."

"Does he know yet?" Hope asked.

"Yeah. I called him. He seemed to take it okay. He was sorry he didn't make it here in time, but he knew it was coming."

Hope rubbed Carrie's leg and wished she could do more to comfort her. "Do you want me to go to the funeral home with you?"

Hope's offer brought fresh tears to Carrie's eyes. "I would love you to go with me. But I'm not exactly sure that would be best for my mom. Is that all right?" Hope looked into Carrie's eyes. Hope knew she was worried about her feelings. Her grandmother had just died, yet she was worried about Hope. The care she showed seeped into Hope's heart and warmed her.

"Of course, it's all right, honey."

"But…" Carrie hesitated. "Would you come to the funeral with me? I think it would help a lot if you were there with me."

"Absolutely." Hope wrapped her arms around Carrie and pulled her in close. She held her for a long time, rubbing her back, and trying to smooth away some of the pain.

CHAPTER TWENTY-SIX

Hope checked her cell phone for the tenth time. No missed calls, no message from Derrick. She had called him three times and still hadn't heard back from him. She talked briefly to Erin just to make sure they were both all right. Erin assured her they were, and she would tell Derrick to return her call.

Hope opened her laptop and searched her brain for just the right words to say. She knew she needed to get through to her son and get the lines of communication opened again. She stared at the screen for quite a while before she typed.

Derrick,
I'm sorry I got so upset with you. It is only because I love you and want you to have the best life possible. So, when I think you aren't making the best decisions, it scares me. I don't ever want you to struggle or be unhappy. I'm not mad at you or at Erin. I want the best for you both. Please call me, I promise to listen this time. I don't want this to come between us.
Love,
Your Crazy Lesbian Mama

She reread the email and hit send.

The next morning, she was dressing for Carrie's grandmother's funeral when her cell phone rang. She saw her son's name pop up on her caller ID.

Butterflies took up residence in her stomach. She pushed talk. "Hi, honey. How are you doing?"

"I'm okay." His voice sounded strained. "You aren't going to talk me out of marrying Erin."

Hope closed her eyes and took a deep breath. "All right, but I think we should all sit down and talk about this. Are you willing to do that?" Hope waited for his answer, which seemed to take forever.

"Yeah, we can do that. I can't come until Christmas break. So if you want to come here before that you can. Otherwise we have to wait."

"You aren't going to do anything stup—um, *anything* in the meantime. You aren't going to get married right away, are you?"

Hope could hear the annoyance in Derrick's voice. "No, Mom, we aren't going to run off and get married. I want to do this right. Erin deserves a nice wedding."

"Listen, Derrick, I need to get going. Carrie's grandmother died and I have to go pick her up for the funeral. I'll call you tomorrow, all right?"

"Sure," he said. "Tell Carrie I'm sorry about her grandmother."

"I will, honey. I'll talk to you tomorrow then. Love you."

At least they weren't going to do anything too soon. That was a relief. Sort of.

Carrie stood behind a podium at the front of St. Peter's Church and smoothed out the piece of paper in front of her. She had been clutching it so tight through the first part of the funeral that it was a wadded mess. No matter. She knew what she wanted to say. She just wasn't sure she was going to get through it without breaking down. There were several tissues tucked into the sleeve of her black cotton shirt, just like her grandmother had taught her to do when she was a child. She hadn't done it in years. Today, not only would she need a steady supply of tissues, but she also thought it was a fitting way to remember and honor her grandmother.

The church was filled with people who knew and loved her grandmother, and others who were there to support Carrie or her mom. Several of Carrie's friends and coworkers were in attendance. She stole a glance at Hope in the front row, catching her eye and silently thanking her, so glad she was there. The smell of burning frankincense clung to the air making it feel thick and heavy.

Carrie leaned closer to the microphone. "I want to thank everyone for being here today." She cleared her throat and glanced at her notes. "What do you say about someone who was one of the most important people in your life? I can start out by saying I loved my grandmother. Everyone who knew her loved her. She was one of the kindest, most thoughtful people I have ever known. She was truly a gift from God." Carrie paused to take a deep breath and compose herself.

"I was lucky enough to not only have her for my grandmother, she was also my best friend. I grew up next door to Gram and would often go over to her house to spend time with her and see what she was doing. And if you knew my grandmother at all you can guess what she was doing most of the time. Baking."

It felt good to talk about her grandmother and the quiet laugh that emanated from the group touched her heart. "Her specialty was pie. Whenever I showed up at her door, usually unannounced, she never told me to go away or treated me like a little kid. She always welcomed me with open arms. When she wasn't baking she was out helping others." Carrie looked out at the crowd. "I see a lot of you nodding your heads. My grandmother touched the lives of so many of you here. She was always sharing her baked goods, volunteering at church, or just helping out a neighbor or a friend." She wiped a tear and continued.

"She married the love of her life when she was only seventeen years old and she had my mother exactly nine months later." Her audience responded with another chuckle.

"I guess we know what she did on her honeymoon." Carrie laughed along with the group despite her tears.

"She was proud of her family and told me often how proud she was of me. She made me proud of myself. She made everyone feel better about themselves. She was a very special lady, my Gram. I was very blessed to have her in my life and I am glad we are all here today to celebrate her life together. I know I am a better person for knowing her." Carrie looked up into the air. "I love you, Gram. I will remember you and miss you always." Carrie wiped a few more tears, folded her notes in half, and took her seat next to Hope. Hope took her hand in both of hers. Carrie was grateful for the warmth and comfort that small gesture gave her. She was so grateful for the woman sitting next to her.

❖

"You did great," Hope told Carrie later. "You did your grandmother proud."

"I appreciate that. And I really appreciate you being with me." She pointed to the left. "Turn here. My mom's house is the third on the right."

"It's obvious your grandmother was loved." Hope parked behind a few cars that were parked on the street. The driveway was full. She rested a hand on Carrie's knee. "Looks like there are a lot of people here already." Another car pulled up behind them. "Are you ready to go in?"

"In a few minutes." They watched as more people made their way into the house.

"Hope," Carrie said. "Would you be okay if I held your hand in there?"

Hope had never even considered this possibility. She'd never been *out* before and took only a moment to consider it. "Of course. I would be very proud to hold your hand and let people know we're together."

Carrie gave her a kiss on the cheek. "Thank you."

"For what?"

"For being you. For caring about me."

"I was born to be me. And caring about you is what I do."

They walked across the lawn hand in hand. Hope wasn't the least bit self-conscious. It felt totally natural. This was who she was, and Carrie was who she loved.

CHAPTER TWENTY-SEVEN

Carrie was glad life was starting to settle down after Thanksgiving and her grandmother's funeral. A quick glance at the clock told her Hope would be arriving soon. She had barely finished the thought when she heard Hope's car pull into the driveway. She opened the door and watched Hope come up the walk.

"Hello, beautiful," Carrie said as Hope approached. She pulled her into a tight hug that ended with a lingering kiss.

"Well, it's nice to see you, too."

"Kitchen. Pie. Pie in the kitchen," Carrie said. Carrie cut them both a slice. They settled down across from each other at the table.

"Mmm," Hope said. "This is so much better than the one I bought for Thanksgiving."

"That's because it's made with love. The pies from the bakery are only made with sugar and love beats out sugar every time."

"This is awfully sweet for not being made with sugar."

"That's because I'm sweet."

"Yes, you are."

"As soon as we finish this pie, I'm going to get you naked," Carrie told her.

"I know you are. But the problem with that is I'm going to be the only one naked."

"I can live with that," Carrie said. "At least for right now."

Carrie put their empty plates in the sink and they made their way to the studio. Carrie stayed while Hope got undressed. She watched her remove each piece of clothing and lay it over the chair in the corner. Carrie couldn't help but look at Hope's body with longing. She knew in a few minutes she would have to stop looking at it with a lover's eye and start looking at it with an artist's eye. She would have to reduce Hope's body to shapes and values.

This was their last modeling session, which was both exciting and a little sad. Hope got into position, standing sideways, her hands hanging by her side and her chin tilted down, toward the left. Carrie came up behind her with the pink satin material in her hand. Each painting featured a different color cloth and Carrie arranged the material over Hope's shoulder and let it drape across one side of Hope's butt. She carefully moved the material around trying to match the placement and folds of the previous modeling sessions.

When Carrie was sure she had the material just the way she wanted it, she leaned in until her mouth was close to Hope's ear. "Just like that," she whispered. "Don't move."

Carrie let her hands sweep down Hope's back with the lightest touch, until she reached Hope's buttocks. She took hold of Hope's flesh and gave a gentle squeeze. Hope shivered.

"You need to stop doing that, unless you want a stream of moisture running down my leg to include in your painting. You're making me very wet."

"Seeing you like this is making me very wet," Carrie responded.

"Do you talk to all your models like this?"

"Yes, I do. Seeing as you are my only model."

Carrie cleared her throat and backed away. "If I don't start painting soon, I'm going to throw you on the floor right here and have my way with you." She turned on the lights to illuminate her subject and sat at her easel. She studied her model, trying to get her brain to see the shapes and light instead of the beautiful body that stood before her. She pushed away her feelings of want and began painting.

❖

"Carrie, I love them. I can't believe how good you made me look." Hope's attention went from one painting to the other.

As pleased as Carrie was with how the paintings turned out, she was even more pleased with Hope's reaction to them. "It was easy to make you look good. All I did was translate your natural beauty to the canvas. Now comes the hard part."

Hope turned her attention to Carrie. "What's that?"

"I have to package them up and send them away. The show in New York City starts December twentieth. I have to have these there by the end of the week. I'm so glad I decided to go with the two-inch gallery wrapped canvas, so I don't have to frame them."

"Whatever that means, they look great."

Carrie laughed but took the time to explain it to Hope. She pulled a sturdy wooden box and a roll of bubble wrap out of the closet. "Want to help me package them?"

"Of course. Just tell me what to do."

They worked side by side, carefully wrapping and boxing the paintings. Carrie felt a loss as they closed the box. She'd spent a lot of time with these paintings. As stupid as it sounded, even in her own head, each painting was a piece of her, an offspring of sorts. Most of her paintings were created not only from her heart but also with the hopes of selling somewhere down the road. Carrie was proud of all her past sales and the fact they had found new homes and new people to love them. Somehow these two paintings were different. Carrie had more than just her heart in these, she also had a piece of her soul.

She'd struggled with the thought of selling them. In the end she decided to put a price on the first one but listed the second as not for sale. She had no problem putting it in the art show, that was a good way to get commissions, but she also looked forward to getting it back at the end of the show. She already had a spot on her bedroom wall in mind to hang it.

"Is it hard for you to send your babies so far away?" Hope said.

Carrie chuckled. "Get out of my head. I was just thinking about that. It is. Probably not as hard as it was sending Derrick away to college, but not easy."

"That," said Hope, "was not hard. I love him of course, but it was nice getting my life back. It helped that he was only an hour and a half away. Might have been a different story if he had gone halfway across the country. I still get to see him on a regular basis." She put her arm around Carrie's shoulder. "When you sell a painting do you miss it?"

"I know it sounds silly, but I do. I always take pictures, so I guess I could make prints if I wanted to."

"Is there going to be a big opening for the show in New York City?" Hope asked.

"Yep." She'd attended openings in the past. But somehow, she didn't feel like going to this one. Not alone anyway. With everything Hope was going through with Derrick, it didn't seem right to ask her. She was grateful when Hope didn't ask any further questions.

"Want me to go with you to drop this at UPS?"

"I would appreciate that."

They loaded the paintings into Carrie's back seat. Carrie wasn't the least bit self-conscious when she kissed her fingertips and touched the top of the box before the customer service rep took the box away.

She might have sent her paintings out into the great unknown, but she still had the subject of her paintings by her side. Hope. She was looking forward to going into the great unknown with her.

CHAPTER TWENTY-EIGHT

Carrie flipped a piece of French toast in the pan. For someone who didn't cook, Hope certainly had nice cookware.

"You look so cute in my clothes," Hope said. "But just so you know, I emptied out a couple of drawers in my dresser if you want to bring some of your clothes to leave here."

Carrie was touched. She looked down at the faded old T-shirt and sweatpants she'd slipped on when she got out of Hope's bed that morning.

"How are you doing?" Hope asked.

"I still find it hard to believe Gram is gone. But I'm hanging in there. How are you? What are you going to do about Derrick?"

"What can I do?" Hope set the table for breakfast. "He has a mind of his own, and I don't think I'm going to be able to change it. I am going to wait until he comes home for Christmas break, and I'll talk to him and Erin and try to convince them to at least wait a while before they get married."

"The baby won't wait." Carrie wanted to tread lightly. "How are you feeling about that part of all this? The baby part?"

Hope put a napkin at each setting and placed a fork and knife on top of it. "To be honest, I haven't really thought about the baby part. I have been so wrapped up in the marriage part."

"Grandma," Carrie said in a hushed voice with a smile.

"Grandma?" Hope repeated. "I'm not sure I like grandma. I'm way too young for that."

"Way too sexy, too." Carrie set the French toast on the table and wrapped her arms around Hope from behind and rested her chin on Hope's shoulder. "How about Nana? Or G-ma. Oh, I like that. It's young. It's hip. It's modern. G-ma. Come on say it with me. G-ma."

Hope turned so they were face-to-face. "You're crazy, you know."

"You don't like G-ma? I like it."

Hope gave her a kiss on the nose. "I like you. G-ma, I'm not so sure of." She raised Carrie's chin and kissed her on the mouth lightly. "Can we eat? That food smells great and I'm starving."

Carrie swatted her on the butt. "Is that all you ever think about? Food?"

Hope pouted. "No." She counted off on her fingers. "I also think about sex…and you…and sex with you." She pulled out a chair for Carrie. "That's all I think about, food, sex, and you. Not necessarily in that order."

"I said it the first time I met you, and I'll say it again."

"That I'm really pretty, super smart, and sexy, too?" Hope grinned.

"No, I was thinking more along the lines of you being a smart-ass."

"Oh yeah, that's me. I'm a smart-ass. That's for sure. I see you used one of the *good* pans."

"I hope that's okay. I probably should have asked first."

"No, I love that they are finally getting some use. In fact you can use them as often as you want."

"Gee, thanks," Carrie said with a grin. "I asked you a little while ago. Have you had time to think about the answer?"

"What was the question again?"

"How do you feel about the baby?" Carrie poured herself another cup of coffee. She held the pot up and nodded toward Hope's cup.

Hope peered in. "Nope, I'm fine."

"So...the baby?"

"I'm sure I'll love the baby. I don't think that will be a problem. And it really doesn't bother me to be a grandmother." She stopped and seemed to gather her thoughts. "I think Derrick will make a great father. He has always loved children and been really good with them. All of the neighborhood kids would come over here to hang with him, even when he was a teenager." Hope laughed. "I remember, not that long ago, Derrick must have been about sixteen at the time. There was this little tiny knock on the door. I wasn't even sure at the time that I had heard it. Well, anyway when I opened the door, there stood the cutest little boy. He couldn't have been any older than six or seven. He looked at me with big wide eyes and asked, 'Can Derrick come out to play?'"

Carrie joined Hope at the table. "Awww, that's sweet."

"Derrick didn't just brush him off like most teenagers would have. He asked him in and got some of his old puzzles out. They sat together for hours at the kitchen table putting them together and drinking cocoa."

"Derrick sounds like a special kid," Carrie said.

"He is. But it's the kid part that has me so worried. He's still just a kid himself."

"Having a baby can make him grow up fast."

"Too fast. I can attest to that. I had all these responsibilities that were way too much for a teenager to handle."

"Don't forget you had an extra burden, making it even harder for you," Carrie said. She took Hope's hand in hers. "You had the burden of trying to hide who you really were. You had to pretend to be something you weren't."

"I don't think Derrick is doing that. I have been pretty good at reading my son and I think he really loves Erin. But playing grownup when you are so young is hard. I don't want him to miss out on life."

"He's not going to miss out on life. He's just not going to have the neat, little, packaged life you had planned for him. He'll be okay." Carrie gave her a reassuring smile. "From what you've told me, he's a smart kid."

"Apparently, not smart enough to use a condom." Hope laughed.

"Good to see you can laugh about it."

"It's either laugh or cry. So I guess laughing is better."

"Laughing is definitely better," Carrie said. "This will all work out, honey. Somehow."

CHAPTER TWENTY-NINE

It had been a particularly hard day for Carrie. She missed her grandmother and just couldn't get out of the funk she was in. Work was a struggle, so she left early and spent most of the day crying. The doorbell rang, forcing her to get off the couch where she had planted herself hours earlier so she could have her own personal pity party. She was happy to see Hope standing there when she opened the door.

"Hi," Carrie said. "What are you doing here?"

"Does that mean you're glad to see me?"

Carrie pulled Hope into a hug. "Of course I'm glad to see you. You just don't usually come over this early on a weekday. How come you aren't at work?"

"I got out early. We had a slow day and I kind of, somehow, sort of lied and told them I had a headache. I felt like I needed to be with you, and from the amount of used tissues on this coffee table, I'd say I was right." They sat on the couch and she rubbed Carrie's knee. "Not doing too good today, huh?"

"I seem to be all over the place with my emotions this week. I miss my grandmother. I know I haven't really had her for a while and I knew she wasn't going to wake up, but I guess a little part of me was really *hoping* she would. I know that sounds stupid."

"Not at all, honey."

"It's like her dying left a hole in me. Sometimes the hole feels really small, like it's hardly there, and sometimes the hole feels so big, I'm sure it's going to swallow me alive."

"I'm so sorry you have to go through this," Hope said. "Is there anything I can do to help?"

"You just being here helps. A lot."

"I could cook us supper. Have you eaten today?" Hope got up.

Carrie laughed out loud. "I know you aren't a fan of cooking. You want to cook now?"

"I said I *would* cook. Not that I *wanted* to cook. I can order delivery pretty darn good. Want me to order us some pizza or Chinese food? Or I can run out and get something, anything you want."

Carrie opened her arms to Hope. "All I really want at the moment is to have you hold me." Hope obliged and pulled Carrie into her arms. Carrie laid her head on Hope's chest and was comforted by the sound of her heart beating.

They stayed like that until it started to get dark outside. "I'm getting hungry. Did you still want to cook for me?" Carrie said.

"Sure. What have you got in the kitchen for me to make?"

"A phone," Carrie said.

"Huh?"

"My phone is in the kitchen. You can use that to order delivery. I'm a little afraid to eat what you might cook." Carrie grinned shyly.

"Hey. I've cooked. It was a long time ago, but I cooked. Um, I remember it had marshmallows and chocolate and crackers. Graham crackers, if I'm not mistaken."

Carrie cocked her head and raised one eyebrow.

"What?" Hope asked. "I did."

Carrie smiled. "S'mores? You cooked s'mores?"

"Yeah, I was twelve and at Girl Scout camp."

Carrie swatted at her. "You are so crazy. Go order me a pepperoni pizza and some mild chicken wings, woman." Hope was halfway to the kitchen. "The pizza menu and phone number are attached to the refrigerator with a magnet." Carrie called to her.

"Boy, you're bossy," Hope yelled back.

She was only gone a few minutes when she returned with a glass of red wine and handed it to Carrie. "Here you go. I thought this would go well with the color of your nose."

"I must look terrible, huh?"

"You look beautiful." Hope settled down next to her and kissed her on the forehead. "The pizza should be here soon."

"Thank you for ordering food, for being here, and for caring."

"Caring about you is the easy part." She put her arm around Carrie. "Ordering that food was the hard part." She looked at her own fingers. "I think I broke a nail dialing that phone."

"Sorry about that. I'll make it up to you later." Carrie snuggled into Hope, careful not to spill her wine.

Hope took the wine glass, sipped from it, and made a face. She handed it back to Carrie.

"Did you just drink some of my wine?" Carrie couldn't hide her surprise.

"Yeah, just thought I'd try it."

"And?"

"And, I still don't like it."

"Maybe you'll like it better when you grow up."

"Maybe. You know what I want to be when I grow up?" Carrie snuggled in closer. "What?"

"A writer."

"You already are a writer." Carrie said. She tilted her head toward Hope and waited for Hope to bring her lips down. They shared a tender kiss.

"I'll accept that. I want to take the next step. I want to be a *published* writer. I sent several of my poems and short stories to some magazines this week."

Carrie pulled back so she could look Hope in the eye. "Oh my God, sweetie, I am so proud of you." She kissed her full on the mouth. "That was a big step."

"I couldn't have done it without you."

"Yes, you could. I just believed in you."

"Like no one ever has before. And I appreciate that."

"I was wondering," Hope said. "What are you planning for Christmas?"

"Well, I was hoping to be able to spend at least part of the day with you. My mother is going to visit my brother in North Carolina for the holidays. They invited me too, but I..." Carrie stopped.

"You what?"

Carrie's cheeks warmed with embarrassment. "I wanted to be closer to you. I didn't like the thought of you being here and me being there. Even if I don't get to see you, I wanted to at least be in the same town." She shook her head. "I know, I know, that sounds all mushy and corny."

Hope took her hand. "No, I think that sounds all romantic and nice." She kissed Carrie's hand. "Could you get any time off from work at Christmas time?"

"I get four days off, but I have plenty of vacation time I could use."

"Think you can take three weeks off?" Hope asked.

"Yeah. Why?"

"Because I wanted to book us a two-week cruise over the holidays. I know the art show in New York City starts soon. I was thinking we could drive there in time for the opening, check out the show, and then fly out of JFK to Florida a couple of days later. The cruise ship departs from there."

Carrie was momentarily speechless. Truly touched.

"What do you think?"

"What about Derrick?"

"I'm not inviting him. It wouldn't be nearly as romantic if we had to share a cabin with him." Hope laughed.

"No. I mean isn't he coming home for Christmas? Don't you want to be with him?"

"He's coming home for two days at the beginning of his holiday break and then he is going home with Erin and spending the rest of his Christmas vacation with her and her family. So it's just you and me, baby. What do you say? Do you think you could put up with me for three solid weeks of togetherness?"

Wow. I could put up with you for so much longer than that. "Hmm, I'm thinking yes. I would love that."

"Good, then that's your Christmas present—a cruise and me."

"Oh, I can't wait to unwrap that present."

"Maybe I'll give you a little preview," Hope said.

"I would like that," Carrie said. In fact, she was looking forward to it.

CHAPTER THIRTY

Derrick leaned his chair back, balancing it on its back legs. Hope looked at the chair legs then back at Derrick. "Sorry," Derrick said, setting all four legs back on the floor. "Erin said to tell you she's sorry she couldn't come. She isn't feeling great and didn't think an hour-and-a-half car ride was a good idea."

It was just as well. It was really Derrick Hope needed to talk to. Although at some point she did want to get Erin's thoughts on everything that was going on.

Hope had taken time to compose herself for this conversation. Carrie had gone over several key points with her. She was calm, composed, and ready. "Tell me what your plans are."

Derrick looked determined and Hope could tell he was trying to control his temper. "First off, we *are* getting married and we *are* raising our baby together. We have already checked into an off-campus apartment. I got a job doing maintenance for them, so the rent is free." Derrick seemed to be watching Hope keenly for her reaction. "I can still go to all my classes. They know I am a full-time college student." Derrick answered her question before she got a chance to ask it. He was well rehearsed and had obviously practiced exactly what he was going to say.

"And Erin?"

"She's happy about this. She'll finish out this year. We get out of school for the summer in May. The baby is due at the beginning of July. She's going to take one semester off and then go back to school in January. And before you ask, we also checked out day care. They have a program through the college. Erin is gonna work there one day a week. That will give her more time with the baby and it lowers the cost. We are both trying to get part-time jobs to pay for food and baby stuff. Erin might have to wait until after the baby is born. We aren't sure about that part, yet."

Hope had to admit she was impressed by the research and plans Derrick had made. She wasn't quite prepared to say that to him, yet. It didn't make her worry less but at least he had put thought into this. He wasn't going in blind like she had. "So what happens in the summer? Will the two of you be coming here to stay?"

"We're going to stay in Buffalo. That way we keep the apartment and Erin's mother is close by. She lives in Cheektowaga, about twenty minutes away." Hope couldn't help but think how grown up her baby sounded.

"What does Erin's mother think about all this?" Hope asked.

"She reacted pretty much like you did. She's worried and she's pissed." Derrick started to lean back in his chair again and stopped, bringing the chair back to the floor. "She's dealing with it. She wants to be there for Erin and the baby."

Hope didn't have any argument left in her. "Sounds like you've thought this out, but do you realize how hard it is to be married and to be a parent? Have you thought about that part, Derrick?"

"Yeah, I think I have. I think I can be a good father because I learned from the best. I guess I will just have to learn the rest as I go. Isn't that what you did?" He paused and put his hands out.

"And look how great I turned out." His smiled, showing a set of perfectly straight teeth. Two years of wearing braces definitely paid off. Thank God Hope got a discount. "I just want you to be happy for me, Mom, because I'm really happy about this."

"I know. It's just really hard for me. I went through this, Derrick. It's difficult. I just wanted to protect you from that." Hope shook her head.

"You can't protect me from life, Mom. This is *my* life. This is what I want."

"All right. I know there isn't anything I can do at this point. Can you just give it some time and not get married right away?"

"We want to get married in May right after the semester ends. We're thinking a small wedding. Just a few friends and family."

That was still more than five months away. Not as far away as Hope had wished, but it wasn't tomorrow either. She just had to believe Derrick would have it better than she did. The fact that he and Erin loved each other put them ahead of where she had started.

Hope stood and motioned for Derrick to do the same. She gave her baby boy a hug. He stood a good five inches taller than her, but he would always be her baby. "I just need time to process this. All right? I just need a little time."

"I figured you would," Derrick said. "Now what do you have in the house to eat? I'm starving."

Some things never changed.

❖

"It went okay with Derrick?" Carrie asked Hope later that day.

"Yes. As well as it could under the circumstances. It sounds like he and Erin have thought about this and are taking steps in the right direction to make it work. So, I decided I'm not going to worry anymore."

Carrie laughed. "And how is that working for you?"

"Not good. I still worry. It's just so hard to make a marriage work and being so young, it is going to be even harder."

They were sitting on a wooden bench in the mall, taking a break from Christmas shopping. Santa sat on his fancy gold chair, not far away. Hope watched as the children lined up to tell him their Christmas wishes.

"Do you think it was extra hard for you because you didn't love Tom, or do you think it's that hard anyway?" Carrie asked her.

"Both," Hope answered honestly. She smiled as she watched a little boy trying to climb up on Santa's lap. It wasn't that long ago that Derrick was that age doing the same exact thing.

"What if *we* were married? Would it be so hard?"

"If you and I were married?"

"Yes, what if you and I were married?"

Hope thought about it. "I don't think that would be so hard." She loved being with Carrie and spending her life with her, well, that was something Hope could see herself doing. That would be so different than it was with Tom.

"And why is that?" Carrie asked.

"Because of how much I care about you," Hope said sheepishly. "All right, it was harder for me because I didn't love Tom. But it's still hard work. I hope Derrick and Erin are up to it. I keep going back to the same thing in my head. They are both so young."

Carrie stood, grabbed Hope's hand, and pulled her up. "Come on," she said. "We are going to go look at baby clothes. They make the cutest stuff nowadays. There's a great store in here. I bought a bunch of stuff for my niece and nephew."

Hope started to protest but decided Carrie was right. There was a baby coming, and looking at baby things would probably be fun. She might even buy something for her new grandchild if anything caught her eye. *My grandchild.* She rolled the thought around in her head as Carrie pulled her around the corner to Lots of Love Baby Stuff. A beautiful little baby boy or girl. A new little person she could love. She followed Carrie into the store and picked up a tiny pair of canvas sneakers. She held them out for Carrie to see and smiled. Yeah. Maybe she could do this.

CHAPTER THIRTY-ONE

Hope placed the silverware on the table and ran a nervous hand through her hair. Hope yelled to Derrick to turn down the volume on his video game—for the third time.

On the stove was the only thing Hope could cook with any confidence, spaghetti and meatballs. The sauce was from a jar, but Hope had used that brand many times before and it always came out fine. The pot of water was just starting to boil. She turned the flame under the sauce and meatballs down.

"Hi," Carrie said.

Hope jumped, turned, and put her hand over her heart. "You startled me. I didn't hear you come in."

"Hey. You shouldn't have given me a key if you didn't want me to silently let myself in and sneak up on you."

Hope gave Carrie a kiss on the cheek. "That's the exact reason I gave it to you. Want some wine?"

"No," Carrie said, holding up a heavy plastic bag. It looked heavy. "I brought soda pop. Where's Derrick?"

"He's in the family room. Can't you hear the video game?" Hope added salt to the now fully boiling pot of water.

"Yeah, I can hear it. I just thought someone was in your house shooting a machine gun." Carrie poured two glasses of ginger ale. "Want some help?"

"No." Hope put her hands on her hips. "I am perfectly capable of cooking us a meal." *I think.* What she lacked in cooking skills she made up for in fake confidence.

"I have total—partial—faith in you and your cooking abilities," Carrie said with a wink.

Hope opened the box of pasta, spilling a few pieces on the floor. She dumped the rest of the box into the pot of boiling water and stirred it. "I've got it," she said when Carrie bent to pick up the pieces from the floor.

"You're nervous, aren't you?" Carrie asked.

Hope picked up the pieces of pasta she'd spilled and deposited them in the trash can under the sink. "How did you know? Does it show?"

"No. I just know you and I can tell."

"This is the first time you and Derrick have spent any time together. I want the two of you to get along. More than that. I really want you to like each other. Are you nervous at all?" Hope asked her.

Carrie let a beat go by before answering. "Let's see. I care about you. And you care about Derrick. I'm sure I'll care about Derrick and look at me." Carrie put her arms in the air. "What's not to love?"

Hope put her arms around Carrie and kissed her. "There is nothing not to love. I think."

"You think?"

"Yeah. You can never be too sure."

"Smart-ass."

"How come you are always talking about my ass?"

"Cause it's so darn cute."

Carrie pulled Hope closer to her and gave her a passionate kiss. Which Hope gladly accepted and returned.

"How come every time I walk into a room, I see something I shouldn't?" Derrick asked, leaning against the doorjamb.

"Because you just walk in without any warning," Hope said. She returned to the stove and stirred the sauce, a little embarrassed at being caught.

"Should I yell 'I'm coming in!' before entering any room in the house?"

"Something like that, smart-ass." *Apparently, the nut didn't fall far from the tree.*

"Hey, Derrick, how are you doing? I brought soda. Would you like some?"

"Hi. Sure, I'll get it." He poured himself a glass and sat at the table.

Hope turned to catch them watching her. "It's hard enough for me to cook in general. It's harder with an audience. This will be ready in about ten minutes. The two of you go watch TV or play a video game. Anything. Just do it in another room."

"Sure, Mom. I'm going into the living room now," Derrick yelled. "How's that? I warned everyone I was going into the living room."

"Good job, smarty."

The two left the room and Hope could hear the television set turn on.

Derrick plopped down on the couch, television remote in hand. "Anything you want to watch?" he asked Carrie.

Carrie sat on the other end. "Whatever you want is fine." They sat in silence for several long moments—very long moments as Derrick flipped through the channels.

"It's very important to your mom for the two of us to get along. I would like that, too," Carrie said.

"I know." He seemed to keep his attention on the TV screen.

"You need to know I'm crazy about your mother and I want her to be happy."

"I want her to be happy too. I just don't want her to get hurt."

"I don't plan on hurting her. I will do my best to make sure that never happens. I promise you."

He finally turned and looked at her. "I guess me and you got no problems then."

Carrie wasn't used to being around teenagers, but she didn't think he was being sarcastic. It was a start. Of course, Derrick would be worried about his mother. It only made sense. She'd been through so much.

Several minutes later, Hope called them to eat.

"I'm coming into the dining room now," Derrick yelled a moment before he walked into the room.

Hope set a plate of garlic bread on the dining room table. "Okay, Derrick, very funny. Sit down and eat. Carrie sit here." She pulled out a chair for her.

"Thanks," Carrie said. "Everything looks good."

"Don't sound so surprised." Hope smiled. "I'm pretty sure it's edible."

"I'm sure it'll be great," Carrie said. "It smells really good." She put a heaping mound of spaghetti on her plate and added a meatball. She passed the bowl to Derrick and took a bite of her food. "Mmm, this is good, Hope."

"Yeah, it is, Mom," Derrick added.

"Thanks." Hope passed around the plate of garlic bread. "Derrick, tell Carrie about your art class at school. She's an artist you know."

"It's a figure drawing class. We did some gesture drawings the other day. We get to work from a live model. It's actually pretty cool."

"That's great," Carrie said. She glanced at Hope.

"Carrie does oil painting. She did two figure paintings using me as a model. They are going to be in a show in New York City soon."

Derrick looked from Hope to Carrie. Carrie tried to read his face.

"Isn't that great?" Hope added.

"Yeah, that's really cool. Is it at some sort of museum or something?"

"It's at a gallery in Manhattan. I've had several of my paintings in exhibits there before," Carrie answered.

"Cool."

"So, where is Erin, Derrick? How come she didn't come with you for this visit?" Carrie asked him. This seemed to be going well. Carrie caught Hope's eye and couldn't help but notice the smile on her face.

"She's been throwing up so she went to her house. Her mom wanted to help and take care of her. I'm going there tomorrow, and spending Christmas with them. Mom told me you guys are going on a cruise for Christmas."

"Yeah. I'm really looking forward to it. I've never been on a cruise before," Carrie said.

"It should be very exciting," Hope added.

"Me and Mom and Dad went on a cruise when I was ten. It was really fun."

"Where did you go?" Carrie asked him. She winked at Hope to let her know it was okay for him to talk about Tom. She got a thankful smile in return.

"The Caribbean," Hope answered for him.

"I can't wait to go." She rubbed Hope's knee under the table and smiled at her.

"What classes are you taking besides art?"

Derrick filled her in between bites.

❖

"That went well," Hope said as she wrapped the leftovers and Carrie loaded the dishwasher.

"I think so."

Hope grabbed her by the waist and pulled her into the pantry.

"Hey. What are we doing?"

Hope shut the door and pushed Carrie up against it.

"Whatever it is, I like it," Carrie said.

"I'm going to kiss you and I don't want Derrick walking in on us again."

"Oh yes. I do like—" Her words were cut off as Hope's mouth crushed into hers.

Carrie had trouble catching her breath by the time they came up for air. "Is this because I was nice to your son?"

"No. That's just because. This is because you were nice to my son." Hope kissed her again.

"Remind me to be nice to him more often." It had turned out to be a very nice evening. Then of course any evening with Hope was special. And Carrie was looking forward to many more.

CHAPTER THIRTY-TWO

Hope took the sheet of paper out of the printer, folded it, and put it in the envelope that had arrived in yesterday's mail. She tucked it into the front pocket of her carry-on case and zipped it closed. She packed her clothes into the matching suitcase and tucked in the lacy lingerie she purchased from Victoria's Secret. She smiled at the thought of wearing it for Carrie. Not that she would be wearing it long. She'd never had a desire to put on something sexy to go to bed in before. She definitely had the desire now. Carrie brought out a lot of desires in her.

She finished packing, lugged the suitcase and carry-on down the stairs, set them by the front door, and took a mental inventory. *Bags are packed and ready to go. Timers on the lights are set so it looks like someone's home. Thermostat is set lower. Back doors are locked. Front door gets locked when I leave. Anything else I'm forgetting? No, I think that's it.* She'd already talked to her neighbor about getting her mail and watering her plants.

She put on her coat and gloves and headed out the door grateful her suitcase was on wheels. Her breath was visible in the bitter cold air. She would be in warmer weather soon enough. Frigid air shot out of the heater as soon as Hope started the car. She quickly turned the fan off to stop the rush and pointed her car in the direction of Carrie's house. The drive to New York City was a good six hours, as long as there were no delays. She was actually looking forward to that much time alone in the car with Carrie with no distractions.

Getting an early start was a good idea. They would have time to settle into the hotel and grab something to eat before the art show opening. Hope was excited to see Carrie's paintings hanging in a gallery. She was so proud of her.

Carrie was all packed and ready to go when Hope arrived. She threw a ziplock bag of cookies into her backpack.

"Got everything?"

"I think so. I'm all ready to spend time with my lady love. That's you."

"Good to know."

They made good time, stopping once to grab something to eat and a couple more times for gas and bathroom breaks.

"How many beds?" the pleasant woman behind the counter at the hotel asked.

Hope glanced at Carrie before answering. "One. A queen or king would be great." Another step in coming out, she thought. It wasn't nearly as hard as she would have thought. Of course, coming out with Carrie by her side made it that much easier. She liked the fact that Carrie let her do it at her own pace.

She did tell a few friends from work and got nothing but support in return. She planned on telling her sister and parents when they returned from their cruise and was sure—almost sure—that she would meet with some resistance, but she would just deal with that. There wasn't much she had done in her life that didn't call for an opinion from her mother and sister. She was used to it and could let it roll off her back. Not that she liked it. They had even objected to her marrying Tom, despite the fact she was pregnant. Okay, they had been right on that one. She'd give them that much. She knew she would have an ally in her father. For that she was grateful.

"Would you like help with your luggage?" The question pulled Hope out of her thoughts.

Carrie piped up. "I think we're all set."

Hope nodded her agreement and handed Carrie one of the two key cards. Not that she anticipated they would both need one. Hope thanked the hotel clerk and grabbed the handle on her suitcase. Carrie led the way to the elevator and up to the fifteenth floor.

Hope flung open the curtains and the room filled with light. "Oh my God, Carrie, look at this view." The city below was bustling, with ant-like people rushing here and there. Above, slivers of bright blue sky filtered in between the tall buildings.

"It's spectacular. As are you." She wrapped her arm around Hope and kissed her cheek.

"I can't believe we are in the City of Angels."

"You are an angel, but I'm afraid that's Los Angeles."

"The City of Dreams?"

"Los Angeles again."

"Salt City? Flour City? Emerald City? The City That Never Sleeps. I knew it the whole time. I was just funning ya."

Carrie's laugh was just the reaction Hope was reaching for. She would never tire of the sound of it.

"What would you like to do now that we are in the City That Never Sleeps?" Carrie asked.

"Take a nap?"

There was that laugh again. "Smart-ass."

"I've never been here before. You have. What do you think we should do?"

"Hmm. There are museums, helicopter tours, the Empire State Building, shopping…"

"Shopping. Let's take a walk and we can duck into any shops that look interesting. What do you think?" She pulled Carrie to her by the waist.

"Anything you want, honey."

They had lucked out on the weather. The sun heated the air just enough to almost be warm and walking knocked out any remaining chill. They strolled for several blocks before stopping at a small boutique. Carrie bought her mother a silk scarf and Hope bought a bib for the baby that said *I'm sick of you people.*

Bring me to Grandma's. She laughed out loud when she read it. Maybe this was going to be all right after all.

Twelve blocks and six stores later, they headed back to the hotel to change for dinner and the art show.

"You look spectacular," Carrie said to Hope. "I have been to a few of these show openings, but I have to tell you I am more excited about this one than any of the other ones."

"Why is that?" Hope slipped her dress shoes on. She'd bought them just for today and had spent hours walking around the house in them to break them in.

Carrie took her hand. "Because I get to walk in with you. Not only am I crazy about you, but I get to show the world how beautiful you are by way of my paintings."

The tender comments went straight to Hope's heart and lit it up. "I am so excited to be sharing this with you. And you look pretty wonderful yourself." She pulled Carrie in for a kiss.

Dinner was everything Hope expected dinner at an elegant restaurant in New York City would be. They had no trouble hailing a cab after and were safely deposited in front of the Marcus Simmons Gallery.

Hope could see through the large window that there was an impressive number of people milling about inside. "Nervous?" she asked Carrie.

"Excited. Thank you so much for sharing this with me and making it possible."

"I wouldn't have missed it for the world. It's kind of cool having a famous artist for a girlfriend."

Carrie laughed. "Not sure I'm famous…" She paused before adding, "yet."

"Just a matter of time baby."

Carrie took Hope's hand. "Here we go." She led the way through the large glass door.

"Carrie Martin," a man dressed in a three-piece suit exclaimed with a flamboyant flair. He pulled her into a hug.

"Not famous, huh?" Hope whispered.

"Still not famous," she whispered back. "Hope, this is Marcus Simmons. He's the gallery owner and a wonderful artist in his own right. Marcus, my girlfriend, Hope Garret."

Marcus offered her his hand. "So nice to meet you, Hope."

She shook his hand. "Likewise."

"Where's David?" Carrie asked.

He glanced around the room. "He's around here somewhere."

"David is Marcus's husband," Carrie told Hope.

"Definitely my better half," Marcus said. "Carrie, your paintings are above and beyond impressive this year. And now I see why. You must have been inspired by your lady here." He turned his attention to Hope. "You make a beautiful model, my dear."

The heat rose from Hope's chest to her face and she worried she was turning beet red. "Thank you. But all the credit needs to go to Carrie."

Carrie gave Hope's hand a squeeze. "I agree with you, Marcus. The model makes all the difference."

"Have a look around. We got a great array of artwork for this exhibit." With that, Marcus disappeared as quickly as he had appeared.

"That was Marcus," Carrie said with a laugh.

"Yes. I gathered that. He seems like a nice guy."

"The best. Want to look around?"

"Absolutely."

There was quite a range of artwork hanging on the multitude of walls and on pedestals and tables in between. Hope couldn't believe all of the different styles and sizes. Some bordered on abstract with just the hint of a human figure, while others were so detailed they looked like photographs.

They rounded yet another corner and there they were. Carrie's paintings. Larger than the ones surrounding them, and maybe she was biased, but more impressive as well. There were several people surrounding them. Hope strained to hear what they were saying. Apparently, they were just as impressed with Carrie's work as she was.

She and Carrie waited patiently for the group to move on before stepping closer. It didn't matter that Hope had already seen the finished paintings at Carrie's house. Seeing them here, on display with so many other pieces of art made them seem different. Better. More important.

Hope pointed to one of the tags proudly displacing Carrie's name and the painting's details. "What's this mean? NFS?"

"That means it's not for sale."

Hope was surprised. "I thought the purpose was to sell your paintings and make money."

"Not this one. This one is special. I couldn't bear to part with it." She turned to Hope. "It's almost as special as you are."

Hope kissed Carrie on the mouth, not caring who saw them. "Thank you."

"Do you know what this means?" Carrie pointed to the red dot on the tag for her other painting.

"No idea."

Carrie smiled. "It means it's sold."

Hope sucked in a large breath. "Oh my God, Carrie. That's so exciting. I'm so proud of you."

"Excuse me." Hope hadn't noticed the couple standing behind them.

"Oh sorry," Hope stepped out of the way.

"No, no," the woman said. "We were just wondering if these paintings are of you. They are quite lovely."

Hope vacillated between being flattered and embarrassed. "They are," she told them. "This is the artist. Carrie Martin. She's the one who deserves all the credit," she said, taking the attention off of her and putting it where it belonged.

"Lovely," the woman said again, this time to Carrie.

"Thank you. I appreciate that."

"I have to agree with my wife. I am very impressed." The man held out his hand. "Jerrod Goldwin."

Carrie introduced Hope.

"This is my wife, Greta. I own The Wild Works Gallery a few blocks from here." He pulled a business card from his breast pocket and handed it to Carrie. "I would be very interested in displaying your work and maybe setting up your own show. I happen to have an opening for the month of August this coming year."

Hope resisted the urge to jump up and down with excitement. Carrie apparently had more couth. She politely accepted the business card. "I would like that. Thank you."

"Email me your portfolio and we can take it from there," Jerrod told her. "Pleasure to meet you." He nodded to each of them. "Carrie. Hope." And he and his wife continued down the aisle.

"That is so exciting," Hope said, barely able to contain her enthusiasm.

Carrie grinned. "It is isn't it."

"What are you going to do?"

"I'm no fool. I'm going to send him my portfolio."

All in all, it was a very pleasant evening. Carrie received a lot of attention and accolades for her paintings. Hope couldn't have felt prouder. They were both tired by the time they got back to the hotel and fell into bed. But not too tired to make love.

"Famous," Hope whispered to Carrie as she was drifting off to sleep.

❖

Hope had no trouble finding a parking spot in the long-term lot at the John F. Kennedy International airport. Luckily, they didn't have to wait long for a shuttle to take them to the terminal. Their flight to Florida was uneventful and boarding the cruise ship went off without a hitch.

Carrie was impressed with the size of their cabin. She thought it would be tiny, with hardly enough room to move around. She was so glad she'd been mistaken. "This is great," she said to Hope. "I love my Christmas present. Thank you."

"You're so welcome. I'm so happy we are doing this. Two glorious weeks alone together. Well, alone with thousands of other people on this ship." She chuckled.

"I know it's not quite Christmas yet, but can I give you your presents now?" Carrie asked.

"I have a little something to give you too. And something I wanted to share."

"You already gave me this cruise. You didn't have to give me anything else."

Hope shook her head. "It's not much so don't get too excited."

"My turn first." Carrie pawed through her suitcase and pulled out two small, neatly wrapped boxes. She handed the first one to Hope.

Hope sat on the bed and took her time pulling off the tape and the small bow.

Carrie fought the urge to tell her to just rip it off.

Hope opened the wooden box and pulled out the pen Carrie had bought a few months before during their walk on the canal. "Oh, Carrie, I love it." She jumped up and gave her a kiss.

"I'm glad. Here." She handed her another box, smaller than the first. Carrie had gone to several jewelry stores looking for just the right gift.

Hope's face lit up when she opened the box to reveal a delicate gold chain with dangling charm sporting the word *AMAZING!* in twenty-four karat gold with a small diamond in the bottom of the exclamation point. "Wow." She brought her attention from the gift to Carrie.

"I just wanted you to know what I thought about you. You are amazing."

"Thank you."

"I have something for you, too." She then extracted the envelope she'd put in her carry on and handed it to Carrie.

"What's this?" The envelope was addressed to Hope.

"Open it and see."

Carrie pulled the flap of the envelope open and pulled out a neatly typed letter. Carrie read it. "Oh my God. You're having one of your poems published. You're going to be a published author." She gave Hope a tight hug. "I am so proud of you. You did it. See I told you you were good." Her smile was as wide as her face would allow.

She sat on the edge of the bed and reread the letter. The smile overtook her again. "What a great way to start this trip," she said.

"There's something else in the envelope." Hope sat on the bed next to her. "It's a poem. I wrote it for you."

Carrie looked at Hope, deeply touched. She pulled another sheet of paper from the envelope.

Carrie's heart swelled, and her eyes filled with tears as she read.

My hearts been handled carelessly
In ways too ugly to tell
So I've bombed all the bridges and armed the battlements
Safely ensconced in my shell

Like a fugitive
Too combative
This no way to live

Now I wish I could say that I treat myself kind
But that would be a lie
Cause I hold myself tight and grasp and fight and I self-crucify

Can a soft caress bring me happiness
End this loneliness

The only thing I know for sure
To avoid regret and strife
Is to not let fear run and rule your life

I'm going to put my faith in you
I'm going to put my faith in me
I'm going to put my faith in the greater powers that be

I'm going to give up
And surrender to the lessons yet to learn
Because since our first kiss I constantly yearn
And I'm willing to open this door for you
Just walk slowly through

Isn't it time for me to trust again
Let the past go, learn to love again
Maybe this time, I'll be in safe hands

Carrie brushed away a tear as she finished reading the poem and gave Hope a soft kiss on the lips. "I love it," she whispered, "I love you."

Hope smiled at her. "The feeling is very much mutual. I love you too. You showed me who I've always been."

She took Carrie's hand and kissed it, never breaking eye contact. This was going to be the best vacation of her life. And her life with Carrie had just begun. She was sure the best was yet to be.

About the Author

Creativity for Joy Argento started young. She was only five, growing up in Syracuse, New York, when she picked up a pencil and began drawing animals. These days she calls Rochester home, and oil paints are her medium of choice. Her award-winning art has found its way into homes around the globe.

Writing came later in life for Joy. Her love of lesbian romance inspired her to try her hand at writing, and she found her first self-published novels well received. She is thrilled to be a part of the Bold Strokes family and has enjoyed their books for years.

Joy has three grown children who are making their own way in the world and four grandsons who are the light of her life.

Visit her website at www.joyargento.com.

Books Available from Bold Strokes Books

A Far Better Thing by JD Wilburn. When needs of her family and wants of her heart clash, Cass Halliburton is faced with the ultimate sacrifice. (978-1-63555-834-0)

Body Language by Renee Roman. When Mika offers to provide Jen erotic tutoring, will sex drive them into a deeper relationship or tear them apart? (978-1-63555-800-5)

Carrie and Hope by Joy Argento. For Carrie and Hope loss brings them together but secrets and fear may tear them apart. (978-1-63555-827-2)

Death's Prelude by David S. Pederson. In this prequel to the Detective Heath Barrington Mystery series, Heath discovers that first love changes you forever and drives you to become the person you're destined to be. (978-1-63555-786-2)

Ice Queen by Gun Brooke. School counselor Aislin Kennedy wants to help standoffish CEO Susanna Durr and her troubled teenage daughter become closer—even if it means risking her own heart in the process. (978-1-63555-721-3)

Masquerade by Anne Shade. In 1925 Harlem, New York, a notorious gangster sets her sights on seducing Celine, and new lovers Dinah and Celine are forced to risk their hearts, and lives, for love. (978-1-63555-831-9)

Royal Family by Jenny Frame. Loss has defined both Clay's and Katya's lives, but guarding their hearts may prove to be the biggest heartbreak of all. (978-1-63555-745-9)

Share the Moon by Toni Logan. Three best friends, an inherited vineyard and a resident ghost come together for fun, romance and a touch of magic. (978-1-63555-844-9)

Spirit of the Law by Carsen Taite. Attorney Owen Lassiter will do almost anything to put a murderer behind bars, but can she get past her reluctance to rely on unconventional help from the alluring Summer Byrne and keep from falling in love in the process? (978-1-63555-766-4)

The Devil Incarnate by Ali Vali. Cain Casey has so much to live for, but enemies who lurk in the shadows threaten to unravel it all. (978-1-63555-534-9)

His Brother's Viscount by Stephanie Lake. Hector Somerville wants to rekindle his illicit love affair with Viscount Wentworth, but he must overcome one problem: Wentworth still loves Hector's brother. (978-1-63555-805-0)

Journey to Cash by Ashley Bartlett. Cash Braddock thought everything was great, but it looks like her history is about to become her right now. Which is a real bummer. (978-1-63555-464-9)

Liberty Bay by Karis Walsh. Wren Lindley's life is mired in tradition and untouched by trends until social media star Gina Strickland introduces an irresistible electricity into her off-the-grid world. (978-1-63555-816-6)

Scent by Kris Bryant. Nico Marshall has been burned by women in the past wanting her for her money. This time, she's determined to win Sophia Sweet over with her charm. (978-1-63555-780-0)

Shadows of Steel by Suzie Clarke. As their worlds collide and their choices come back to haunt them, Rachel and Claire must figure out how to stay together and most of all, stay alive. (978-1-63555-810-4)

The Clinch by Nicole Disney. Eden Bauer overcame a difficult past to become a world champion mixed martial artist, but now rising star and dreamy bad girl Brooklyn Shaw is a threat both to Eden's title and her heart. (978-1-63555-820-3)

The Last First Kiss by Julie Cannon. Kelly Newsome is so ready for a tropical island vacation, but she never expects to meet the woman who could give her her last first kiss. (978-1-63555-768-8)

The Mandolin Lunch by Missouri Vaun. Despite their immediate attraction, everything about Garet Allen says short-term, and Tess Hill refuses to consider anything less than forever. (978-1-63555-566-0)

Thor: Daughter of Asgard by Genevieve McCluer. When Hannah Olsen finds out she's the reincarnation of Thor, she's thrown into a world of magic and intrigue, unexpected attraction, and a mystery she's got to unravel. (978-1-63555-814-2)

Veterinary Technician by Nancy Wheelton. When a stable of horses is threatened Val and Ronnie must work together against the odds to save them, and maybe even themselves along the way. (978-1-63555-839-5)

16 Steps to Forever by Georgia Beers. Can Brooke Sullivan and Macy Carr find themselves by finding each other? (978-1-63555-762-6)

All I Want for Christmas by Georgia Beers, Maggie Cummings, Fiona Riley. The Christmas season sparks passion and love in these stories by award winning authors Georgia Beers, Maggie Cummings, and Fiona Riley. (978-1-63555-764-0)

From the Woods by Charlotte Greene. When Fiona goes backpacking in a protected wilderness, the last thing she expects is to be fighting for her life. (978-1-63555-793-0)

Heart of the Storm by Nicole Stiling. For Juliet Mitchell and Sienna Bennett a forbidden attraction definitely isn't worth upending the life they've worked so hard for. Is it? (978-1-63555-789-3)

If You Dare by Sandy Lowe. For Lauren West and Emma Prescott, following their passions is easy. Following their hearts, though? That's almost impossible. (978-1-63555-654-4)

Love Changes Everything by Jaime Maddox. For Samantha Brooks and Kirby Fielding, no matter how careful their plans, love will change everything. (978-1-63555-835-7)

Not This Time by MA Binfield. Flung back into each other's lives, can former bandmates Sophia and Madison have a second chance at romance? (978-1-63555-798-5)

The Dubious Gift of Dragon Blood by J. Marshall Freeman. One day Crispin is a lonely high school student—the next he is fighting a war in a land ruled by dragons, his otherworldly boyfriend at his side. (978-1-63555-725-1)

The Found Jar by Jaycie Morrison. Fear keeps Emily Harris trapped in her emotionally vacant life; can she find the courage to let Beck Reynolds guide her toward love? (978-1-63555-825-8)

Aurora by Emma L McGeown. After a traumatic accident, Elena Ricci is stricken with amnesia leaving her with no recollection of the last eight years, including her wife and son. (978-1-63555-824-1)

Avenging Avery by Sheri Lewis Wohl. Revenge against a vengeful vampire unites Isa Meyer and Jeni Denton, but it's love that heals them. (978-1-63555-622-3)

Bulletproof by Maggie Cummings. For Dylan Prescott and Briana Logan, the complicated NYC criminal justice system doesn't leave room for love, but where the heart is concerned, no one is bulletproof. (978-1-63555-771-8)

Her Lady to Love by Jane Walsh. A shy wallflower joins forces with the most popular woman in Regency London on a quest to catch a husband, only to discover a wild passion for each other that far eclipses their interest for the Marriage Mart. (978-1-63555-809-8)

No Regrets by Joy Argento. For Jodi and Beth, the possibility of losing their future will force them to decide what is really important. (978-1-63555-751-0)

The Holiday Treatment by Elle Spencer. Who doesn't want a gay Christmas movie? Holly Hudson asks herself that question and discovers that happy endings aren't only for the movies. (978-1-63555-660-5)

Too Good to be True by Leigh Hays. Can the promise of love survive the realities of life for Madison and Jen, or is it too good to be true? (978-1-63555-715-2)

Treacherous Seas by Radclyffe. When the choice comes down to the lives of her officers against the promise she made to her wife, Reese Conlon puts everything she cares about on the line. (978-1-63555-778-7)

Two to Tangle by Melissa Brayden. Ryan Jacks has been a player all her life, but the new chef at Tangle Valley Vineyard changes everything. If only she wasn't off the menu. (978-1-63555-747-3)

When Sparks Fly by Annie McDonald. Will the devastating incident that first brought Dr. Daniella Waveny and hockey coach Luca McCaffrey together on frozen ice now force them apart, or will their secrets and fears thaw enough for them to create sparks? (978-1-63555-782-4)

Best Practice by Carsen Taite. When attorney Grace Maldonado agrees to mentor her best friend's little sister, she's prepared to confront Perry's rebellious nature, but she isn't prepared to fall in love. Legal Affairs: one law firm, three best friends, three chances to fall in love. (978-1-63555-361-1)

Home by Kris Bryant. Natalie and Sarah discover that anything is possible when love takes the long way home. (978-1-63555-853-1)

Keeper by Sydney Quinne. With a new charge under her reluctant wing—feisty, highly intelligent math wizard Isabelle Templeton—Keeper Andy Bouchard has to prevent a murder or die trying. (978-1-63555-852-4)

One More Chance by Ali Vali. Harry Basantes planned a future with Desi Thompson until the day Desi disappeared without a word, only to walk back into her life sixteen years later. (978-1-63555-536-3)

Renegade's War by Gun Brooke. Freedom fighter Aurelia DeCallum regrets saving the woman called Blue. She fears it will jeopardize her mission, and secretly, Blue might end up breaking Aurelia's heart. (978-1-63555-484-7)

The Other Women by Erin Zak. What happens in Vegas should stay in Vegas, but what do you do when the love you find in Vegas changes your life forever? (978-1-63555-741-1)

The Sea Within by Missouri Vaun. Time is running out for Dr. Elle Graham to convince Captain Jackson Drake that the only thing that can save future Earth resides in the past, and rescue her broken heart in the process. (978-1-63555-568-4)

To Sleep With Reindeer by Justine Saracen. In Norway under Nazi occupation, Maarit, an Indigenous woman; and Kirsten, a Norwegian resister, join forces to stop the development of an atomic weapon. (978-1-63555-735-0)

Twice Shy by Aurora Rey. Having an ex with benefits isn't all it's cracked up to be. Will Amanda Russo learn that lesson in time to take a chance on love with Quinn Sullivan? (978-1-63555-737-4)

Z-Town by Eden Darry. Forced to work together to stay alive, Meg and Lane must find the centuries-old treasure before the zombies find them first. (978-1-63555-743-5)